Flight In Time

by

Imogene Nix

LOVE BOOKS

Please note:

The UK and USA share the English language, but there are many words that are spelled differently.

Some words have extra letters in the British spelling, such as the word cancelled. In American English, it is spelled canceled.

There also words that interchange the letters c or s and sometimes z. For example, in America, you spell offense and in Britain, it is written as offence.

We also use the letter u in many words, such as colour and flavour.

These spellings are **not** incorrect.

This book is written in UK English to reflect my Australian/English background.

Ebook: 978-1-922369-78-9

Paperback: 978-1-922369-85-7

Editing by Pamela Tyler

Cover by Dexpress Covers

I'm so glad you could join me for this latest release. I've always wondered what it would be like to be transported to the future, and what better opportunity to test out what we may find? There'd be so many things to learn and experience for the first time, and I hope that's what I've explored in this book.

To mix that along with an opportunity to give the world another romance, well, it makes it all rather satisfying. Of course, this is only the start of a new series and I hope you enjoy it and join me on the ride.

And on that note, in our family, we've been watching the romance of our daughter unfold, and this year, they walked down the aisle. So this book is dedicated to the girl child and her husband (and of course their kitty babies… Eira, Archie and Artis!)

1

The left wing dipped, and Nala clung to the strap of her seat, praying for a safe flight and landing.

Night had settled around the craft hours ago, as they crossed the ocean. Since then, the darkness had been split by tremendous bolts of light. The lightning crashing, the plane buffeted by the winds, and followed by what she was sure was torrential rain.

Others in the back prayed loudly, and the woman beside her sobbed.

Her stomach clenched as she glanced to her side. A light shone through the windows, and she gasped. It grew larger, wider, spinning wildly. Someone screamed as she stared, unable to tear her vision from the growing vortex. In the very centre there was an obsidian darkness. No lights. Just a terrifying blackness.

Engines whined loudly as the hostess called loudly from the front, "Hold on, everyone. Brace yourselves."

Glancing around, Nala noted the varied voices echoing in the cabin. The words 'brace yourself' repeated, and nausea rose, nearly swamping her while her stomach cramped. She moved automatically, hunching forward, her fingers clutching the webbing of her seatbelt. Chill invaded her body, and she shook wildly. Terror kept her eyes wide open, as her brain repeated if the end was coming, she'd face it straight-on.

A flare of light surrounded the small craft, and now she did blink. Suddenly, the craft was overcome with silence. Every sound stopped, the flash of light disappeared, and they were surrounded by darkness.

The engines had stopped; she knew that as clearly as she could feel the sudden cessation of the throb beneath her feet. Her hand released the strap and she reached for the lap sash. It was still there.

The person in the seat at her side stared at her, mouth agape. "We're going to crash," the woman moaned.

"Just hold tight," Nala murmured, but it was like an invisible hand clutched the craft. Doomed, I'm going to die in this plane in the middle of nowhere and no one will know where I am.

A sound now echoed, like the grinding of metal, and the cacophony of screams began anew as the craft pitched from one side to the other in rapid succession, throwing the passengers against each other and the wall of the plane. She clutched her seatbelt once more and whispered a brief prayer, hoping for forgiveness of her many indiscretions, and hoped someone took note and pity on her soul. Tears burned fiery tracks down her cheeks while the thudding of her heart surely heralded a medical incident.

Then it ceased.

The wild movements stilled.

Silence descended.

"What's happening?" she whispered, and the woman beside her stared as she simply shook her head.

Nala scrabbled for the clasp on her seatbelt then threw it aside. A hand reached out, grabbing hers. Looking down, Nala realised it was her seatmate, who one-handed scrabbled for her belt too. The woman whose hand she grasped, surged up beside her, her grip crushing as Nala called out, "Be quiet everyone. We need to know what's happening!"

Not that it made any kind of impression, as the other passengers screamed and whimpered.

One of the hostesses, the tall one who'd told them to brace, hurried along the aisle, her face pasty white, her hand clasping a ring which Nala had seen hanging not quite fully beneath her uniform. The dim light glittered off the rock, a diamond, Nala thought dimly, in a gold band. "You need to resume your seats," she entreated, but Nala noted that she too grabbed Nala's hand.

Only seconds had passed, but it felt like a lifetime when suddenly the craft lurched and stilled. Lights blasted in through the small portholes, and the trio standing in the aisle turned as one.

The doors blew open and a creature lurched into the craft. It was tall, wearing a suit of greyish-green, and the headpiece held a large screen, though it was opaque, and for an instant Nala wondered what they, the creatures who crowded behind the advancing leader, saw. A bubble of hysteria rose in her chest, but she refused to let it out, some sense warning her now was not the time.

The figure stepped toward the three, followed by others. The one she designated the leader strode up to them, the stride purposeful, and on instinct, Nala nudged both the women behind her. She shook with terror, not quite sure what she was facing or who, but sure that this was the right course of action.

"You are the leader," echoed a voice from the helmet.

"I... No." Her voice shook, but at least she could form a coherent answer, she told herself mentally.

The creature glanced side to side then said, "Come with us," and a hand extended. There was an air of authority about this individual, and Nala immediately knew this wasn't a request she could deny. Stumbling, she followed, not taking the hand offered, while the other two women clung like limpets to one of her arms and hands. The creature grabbed Nala, lifting her from the craft to the floor.

The plane doors opened to a large hanger or complex, her mind couldn't offer any other answer, and many more of the creature hovered, as if waiting.

"What about...?" She swallowed the sudden dry lump in her throat.

"The team will bring them aboard safely."

Aboard? That seemed like a strange word to use. Were they on a boat or some kind of plane? And if so, how could…?

"Be at peace. You are now safe."

Once more she blinked. "Safe?"

The hands released her and reached for the head covering, twisting it up and off until she saw a man within the suit. "Yes. Safe. We nearly lost your craft in the wormhole."

"What?" Words she'd never heard nor understood had her shaking her head. "I don't understand, where are we? Why aren't we still flying?"

The man smiled, his perfect white teeth and tanned skin still a surprise along with the flash of jet-black hair and forest-green eyes. "We saved you. You were caught up in a wormhole flash, and your plane would have crashed if we hadn't retrieved it."

"I have no idea who you are or what you're playing with, but I want to go home," the air hostess muttered, her small cap now askew, and her trim skirt and blouse looked positively rumpled. "I can't…" She dropped, but someone swooped in, catching her before she fell, as did a second, catching Nala's seatmate when she too fainted.

Nala wavered. What was the best course of action? Help these women or deal with the man who'd been confusing her? "I want to go home."

"I'm sorry, ma'am. That's not possible." Unsure what else to do, Nala turned once more to face the leader. "Once we drew you into the Havenspace, the wormhole closed. Access to your time is no longer possible."

Havenspace? Wormhale? "Where are we, exactly?" asked Nala.

"More when, ma'am. We've dragged you into 2654, and if I don't miss my guess, you were from the 1940s?"

"1956," Nala corrected, her mind spinning. "You're telling me we've moved through time and… No, it's not possible."

"It certainly is possible," the man insisted, "and you've done it. Welcome back to the world."

The room or hanger or whatever it was swirled until the light bled away and Nala slumped to the floor.

Alric sighed and lifted the woman in the brown and white dress into his arms and laid her on a medi-bed. The others in the hangar were being loaded up, but something about this woman... She'd shielded the other two clinging to her. She'd demanded answers and even corrected him on his poor guestimate of the year.

He slid a red security band onto her hand and slid orange ones on the other two women as he began moving through the rows of beds, his hands moving over the screen of his reader pad, seeking information. 1956, planes... Ah yes. He found an image and nodded, thankful at least that had quickly been rectified.

"You've found a potential leader?" Shuran, his second-in-command, commented on his choice of banding. "We haven't yet got into the cockpit. It's as if they've barricaded it."

"You should be able to push through it. After all, it's a mid-1950's build super constellation, so the security features are poor," Alric muttered.

"They may be, but the cockpit door won't open," Shuran reiterated.

"Then go through the windscreen."

"And if they're armed?" Shuran pushed.

Alric sighed. "You want me to deal with it?"

Shuran shrugged. "At the beginning of this mission you were pretty clear with us, given the situation."

It wasn't often his offsider shied away from responsibility, but he understood with her particular circumstances that now was not the time to run risks. Alric sighed and opened a flap on his wrist unit, deployed the shielding, and strode to the front of the plane, then slid his helmet back on, ensuring his personal safety.

The cockpit was higher up, and clicking his heels together, he activated the power-rise inserts of his boots. Slowly, he rose until he could glance through the glass at the four men huddled in the cockpit. He could now clearly see what they'd stacked in front to stop the intrusion of his people.

The man that he thought was likely the captain, raised a hand, the pistol in his grip wavering. "You can't enter," he croaked while the other men cowered near the rear cockpit seats.

Alric groaned and hovered in full view. "I will not hurt you, but my people cannot reach you in there. Either clear the door or—"

"No," screeched the man as he waved the pistol wildly.

In slow motion, Alric watched the man squeeze the trigger of the ancient pistol. There wasn't much else to do, so he placed his hand against the glass, which crumpled beneath his touch, and he moved out of the way as the bullet whizzed into the protective bubble surrounding the internal area of the hangar.

The man's eyes widened before he turned scarlet and clutched his chest. Alric shot forward, realising what was happening. Once again, his hand was extended, and he flicked his thumb and a long needle protruded, and he shoved it deep, letting the embedded x-ray guide his moves.

The others in the cabin rose, and Alric growled at them, "Stay still and let me save your captain." They stilled and he breathed deeply, waiting for the beep that told him the medic assist embedded in his suit had completed its task. "Open the door and let my people in. Your captain needs to be in the infirmary," he said, and watched on, pleased, as they sprang into action.

Nala yawned, the grogginess invading her brain, an unwelcome effect of the nap she'd taken on the plane. Only, something niggled at the back of her mind, some unwelcome knowledge.

Cracking open an eye, she glanced out, then sprang upright with a gasp. "Where am I?" Certainly not on the plane. Nala looked around.

The room was cavernous, like a hangar for a plane, yet bigger. She'd seen plenty of them in her early years during the war, assisting both her mother and father. She swiped an unsteady hand over her eyes as a green-bedecked woman ambled toward her.

"Good, you're the first awake. Let's get you up and into the interview cubicle so we can begin the process."

"Process?"

"It's all very simple, dear. Nothing to worry about." The woman exuded a strange kind of confidence that unsettled Nala. She was dressed very strangely too. Pants that fitted tight against her body, with silver markings along the arms. Nala wondered if they were signs of rank.

"Where am I? Who are you, and what happened?" Her hand brushed against her dress, and she groaned, noting the wrinkles.

"My name is Shuran, and I'm the second-in-command to Captain Alric. You're aboard the USF Captivar, and we saved you from a mechanically created wormhole."

Nala slid a hand over her forehead. "What are you talking about? I've never heard of a wormhale, and I have no clue what you're talking about." Confusion was a wave that swamped her.

"Wormhole. But it's okay, it will all be explained later. For now, let's get you up and moving."

Shuran pushed her to rise and head toward rooms at the back. She did glance back a single time, noting the rows of people still supine on the beds. "Will they all be fine?"

"Oh, for sure. They'll wake up soon and be processed too. Now, just step in here." Shuran opened a door and all but pushed Nala inside, then closed the door behind her with a whisper.

Alone in the small room, she glanced around, but the room was alien. There was a table in stark white and two formed chairs, also in white. A box-like thing sat on top of the desk, and she stepped up, touched it with a finger, and it trilled.

Terrified, Nala sprang back, her gaze on the box that made a sound, and cowered in the corner.

A door at the other side of the room slid open, and a man she was sure she'd seen before entered, but fear kept her rooted to the spot.

2

Alric looked at the woman who was trying to squeeze through the wall of the cubicle, and he sighed. I've been here before. Clearly, whatever there was in here terrifying her would continue to be a stumbling block until he explained the what's, where's and why's of her situation.

"Please take a seat," he said, indicating to the seat by the computing unit.

"Who are you, and where am I?" She panted, still very clearly shaken.

"I'll answer those in a minute, but what's your name?" he countered.

"Nala. It's Nala."

"A lovely name," he said and wrote it down on the pad before him. "Do you have a surname?"

She blinked. "Stimson. Nala Stimson."

"Nala, I'm Captain Alric of the USF Captivar. This ship, if you will. I know Shuran, my second, told you a little, but let me explain what happened. Your plane was caught in a wormhole, one that was formed in an irregular manner, and you all would have been lost if we hadn't picked up the interference through a time-space device." He held up a tiny receiver in his hands. "We realised the situation and were able to use the warp to pull the plane and all of you forward to the future."

The woman shook her head. "Time travel is a story. It only exists in cheap penny novels," she breathed.

If only those from the past had been given the opportunities to be educated in the lateral fields of time transference. "It really isn't." He smiled and hoped that might calm her somewhat, given the way she'd turned a peculiar shade of greenish-grey. "Come sit down, and I'll get us some refreshment while you assist me with details."

She moved slightly, and he got the impression that interest warred with the lack of knowledge. He tapped a button on the table, and a chime signalled that the two cold drinks were ready to be dispensed. He waited though, until she perched on the edge of the seat, then slid open the receptacle unit and pulled out two cold drinks of icy spice water.

Alric sipped from his cup and watched as she reached for the other. She'd be thirsty, he knew. It was one of the side effects of the sedative they used after the nervous system overload slump all the designates experienced, but they had long ago learned that those unused to the vagaries of worm-transport reacted best to a period of sedation after the initial event. It seemed the brain couldn't cope in their situations and nothing less than twenty-four hours alleviated the worst of the effects.

"How long was I asleep?"

"Not as long as most of the passengers. You were out for twenty hours. Most won't rise until later today or even tonight."

She nodded. "Where am I?"

"This is my ship, and we're heading for the moon hub we call the Havenspace. You'll be kept here long enough to undertake any initial health checks and until we can understand your educational and transitional deficits."

She frowned, and her brows moved together. "Deficits?"

"Knowledge gaps, things you need to know before joining the population of one of the six united planets."

"Six united planets? I'm sorry, but I'm guessing this is a joke. Some cruel prank—" She made to stand up, but he raised a hand.

"Video overlay, screen two," he commanded, and now, the vision of the planets, a basic education spiel they played for youngsters as part of their initial mandatory citizenship training, flashed on the screen.

"The six united planets that make up our human alliance include Earth, Beta Minor, Lascelles IV, Mars, the Pluto explanatory zone, and Romulus. Each planet contributes to the needs of our society through agriculture, aquaculture, mining, and scientific knowledge. While each planet is technically its own civilisation, defence and medical services are combined for the benefit of all." Images flashed on the screen as the spiel moved on. "Each of the six planets contributes labour and knowledge, building better interstellar transportation, and sending explorers out to meet and make alliances with others of a peaceful nature. We seek other m-class planets suitable for habitation. In this way, the six planets promote peace, harmony, and populate star systems."

"What is this?" She rose again, arms wrapped around herself, pale with wide eyes glancing at the screen. "Nothing man-made is this advanced, nor—"

"Not in your time, no. But the wormhole brought you nearly seven hundred years into the future. We—those who serve with the Haven-space—understand that it's difficult to make a transition, particularly for those who've come so far. But many have made the transition, and very well. Indeed, one who you may have heard of, Amelia Earhart, is now serving on one of this craft." He waited and watched as her eyes widened further.

"But what if I want to go home?" He noted the way her hands balled up, and he gathered she didn't grasp the important information he'd just dispensed.

"That's the one thing you can't do. We haven't yet found a way to travel back in time, only to bring those craft forward." What he didn't tell her was why. She wasn't yet ready to hear the rest of the plan. So many craft went missing, but it was only those containing certain individuals that they were given the green light to save.

She slumped into the chair, and he felt bad for her, but the rules were clear. He needed her now to complete her testing, then prepare her for transitional training.

Nala felt her emotions swamping her. Filling her with a mix of disbelief and terror at his words. "I'm a prisoner? Is this the government? I know things have been tricky since the end of the war, the communists—"

He laughed, shook his head. "No. Communism was finally defeated in the early twenty-third century, after the uniting of the first three planetary bodies."

Defeated? She blinked. "I'm not believing what you're telling me. This is some elaborate hoax, but I don't want to participate. Let me go home. I won't tell anyone…"

"It really isn't," he said and relaxed into his chair as if he'd done this countless times before. "Now then, let's begin your aptitude and educational testing."

He waved his hand over the table, and it lit up. She reared back.

"How did you do that?"

He smiled. "Electronics."

She frowned at the unfamiliar word. "Electronics?"

His hands splayed. "Electronics is a science, one which looks at the development, behaviour, and applications of electronic devices. Like this computer."

Nala leaned forward. "What can your computer do?"

"Many things. I can talk to others…communicate. It also lets me learn information, run diagnostic programs for health, education, and even undertake complex calculations."

What a wonder! She waved a hand at the box on the desk. "So that told you that we…"

"No and yes. We expected another plane. We had the timing wrong." He frowned. "But we saw your craft was in trouble, so we grabbed you. It's our mission."

"To bring planes that are going to crash into the future to save them." Not that she really believed what he was saying. After all, this still was a huge hoax; she was sure.

His cough jarred. "Not exactly. See, we were supposed to retrieve a Captain Stainmar. His work on engine manifolds was a game changer."

She didn't know the name, so waited patiently.

"His work is virtually unknown to the general public, but his loss on August 11, 1942, was a tragedy. We felt if he came forward in time, we may be able to work with him. His plane was lost in the region where we found yours. We thought our calculations were correct, but there was some kind of interference."

Nala waited while he explained.

"We missed by fourteen years. Now Shuran and the team will need to reconfigure for the temporal vibrations, which I think affected our calculations."

"I don't understand any of this. But unless you have some reason for holding me, I'm ready to leave, thank you." Nala rose and smoothed down the skirt of her dress, well aware she looked rumpled, and her hair was probably a fright.

Captain Alric shook his head as he sighed. "It's not that simple, as I've told you. This is not 1956, and you can't go home. I'm sorry." He reached out and took her hand. "You can't go home." He repeated the words, and they struck like a frozen arrow in her chest. "You're here. For good."

This time they held a ring of authenticity, and it swept the oxygen from her chest.

Panic settled in, and she pressed a hand against the rising panic in her chest. "I..." She inhaled but it wasn't enough, she didn't feel her lungs filling. It was like she was suffocating, and she clawed at her chest.

"Wait," he muttered and dragged her close. "Breathe."

Dizziness assailed her, her legs felt like damp rags, and she slumped.

"Dammit." He helped her to the chair, before sliding a mask over her face. "Breathe slowly. In and out."

She did, eyes closed, and focussed on her lungs expanding. Controlling the panic that squeezed her chest.

The frenzied emotions abated slowly, but now she was exhausted. Close to tears and her hands shook as she pushed the mask away. "Why?"

"Why what?" He crouched before her.

"Why would you let me live if I'm out of time?" What benefit could she possibly be in a time so far removed from her own?

"Nala, everyone has a reason for being. I don't know yours and you don't know mine, but the universe made you. Put you in the world for a reason, and that's why you lived. Because you and I and everyone has a purpose. Yours it seems, is here in this time." He shrugged.

It wasn't enough, and she screwed her hands tightly together. "But if I'm however old I am, and out of time, then what do I have to offer to society?"

"What did you do in your own time?"

"I was a nurse," she whispered.

He blinked. "Nurse? Okay, we have medical assistants in our time. I guess it's probably close to the same, except you'd have to fully reskill I suppose." He made a note on the screen and a scrolling mass of words floated up before her.

"How... How did you do that?"

He blinked again. "Do what?"

"The words appeared in the air." She reached out, tentative, an attempt to touch them, but her fingertips merely slid through the words and Nala pulled her hand back as if scorched.

"It's a hologram," he answered. "You'll learn more about those as time goes on. But for now, let's see. Reskilling... There's a ten-month bridging program they'll want you to take, and that is concurrent with on-the-job training. Basic biology should be unnecessary. However, they may want to evaluate that. Mandatory vaccinations for Beta-Gam disease and boosters of all childhood illnesses. You'll need to give a blood sample so they can map any traces of antibodies."

She stared at him. It all seemed so simple. Bloodless. Her life gone in a flick, and replaced by a future alone and friendless. Tears burned but she focussed on willing them away.

"Now, what we need to do is run you through an evaluation program. It will consider your education, your health, and your mental status."

Nala bolted upright. "My mental status?" The words left her aghast.

He raised a hand. "Wait! I think in your time, a mental health issue was considered concerning, right?"

She was lost for words and waited, hands clasped so tightly that they were white with pressure. Mental patients were frequently sent away, subjected to all kinds of treatments, and were considered less than whole... Did he think she...?

"In our time, we have medications and therapies that will allow us to assist and support those who have mental health concerns," he muttered, then shook his head. "I struggle with this situation, I'm sorry. I always forget that earlier there was a stigma attached to such things. Forgive me, it's just not something that is even discussed beyond diagnosis and..." He splayed his hands.

How did she respond? How should she respond? She was at sea with the whole line of discussion, but perhaps if she took control? "I think... perhaps," she stumbled over her words. "We should maybe begin this program thing you're talking about. Who do I need to see?"

He smiled, and she wondered if she'd chosen the right words. "No one to see, Nala. On the screen will come words and phrases. It will ask certain questions and you simply answer in your own voice. The text-to-type input will do the rest. At the end, a blood draw will be taken and analysed. I'll remain in here, if you're comfortable, or I can send someone else..."

She shook her head, unwilling right now to present her weaknesses to another person. He was bad enough, she told herself. "No," she whispered. "Please stay."

3

Alric stayed, though he took great pains not to listen in, unless Nala specifically asked for assistance. He was surprised by the level of answers she provided. Detailed, precise, and educated. She was intelligent and focussed, but that this was clear during what had to be exceptionally difficult circumstances was what really drew him.

Each session lasted fifteen minutes then a drink was offered, along with a five-minute break, and she'd sigh, close her eyes, and rest her head against the back of the conformable chair. Once, she excused herself to use the facilities. They'd been specifically retrofitted to look as archaic as she'd been used to, and it never ceased to amaze him how they'd managed to use those ablutionary items.

"Um, how much longer?" Her voice broke through his thoughts.

"Not much longer now. Then the medical staff will come in and you'll meet with a member of the placement council. He'll arrange lodging until everyone has been processed. Once all your cohort have been processed and the results examined, you'll be assigned to a mentor from our crew."

"I just get assigned? There's no options or...?"

Alric frowned. "Is there someone you'd rather be attached to? No one has ever made a request before but—"

She blushed and he didn't miss the rosy hue on her cheeks. It warmed him inside.

"Gosh, no. I'm sorry. Probably these questions seem tiresome to you." Her fingers twined again, and he was coming to realise that was a sign she was uncomfortable.

"No. Not at all." But the discomfort he was feeling—a very unusual reaction for him—was to the way she was clearly working to control frustration and fear. Most unusually he wanted to soothe those thoughts away, run his hands over her brow and tell her everything would be fine.

The bells tolled, telling him the screen was about to activate again, but before he could speak, she said, "I know, it's about to begin again."

The final batch of questions were rapid-fire, attempting to gain the most honest of answers, those used to discern her mental state, her ability to integrate into their society among other important considerations.

When the session was completed, a soft pink glow filled the room. "What's happening?" she queried, and he smiled.

"It means this aspect of the process is complete." A door to his left slid open. "Here's the medical technician now. They'll take a sample, and within a few minutes, we'll have those answers too, then you'll be escorted to the accommodation pods." He rose and smiled. "I'll see you again once they make the announcements of mentors."

"But... I'm being left here?" Her voice was small, her face pale. She reached out to him.

"You'll be fine. From what I've seen, you'll make a valued contribution to our society, Nala. Now, I must go. I've others to meet with."

"Oh. Of course." She drew her hand back, and her face smoothed out, hiding her emotions, and that... it gutted him. "Thank you, Captain Alric."

The dismissal was clear in her voice, and he bowed low and withdrew. On the other side of the door waited Shuran.

She shook her head when he entered the room. "Thank heavens you're done. The other subjects are just starting to wake. I've allocated the passengers to members of the crew, and they'll be entering the assessment bays within the hour. The med-techs are retrofitting to test for varied viruses and bacteria, and the government wants to know how the hell things went wrong. All leave is in abeyance until we can work out what the situation is with the wormhole technology and how we'll re-attempt the retrieval."

"Good day to you too, Shuran. I'll meet with the-powers-that-be after I complete my data download, but the subjects are yours to attend to. They're the spoils of leadership, and I did tell you when you accepted the promotion that was the case." He grinned.

Shuran had only recently assumed the position of second-in-command and this was her first retrieval mission in the position, but he'd personally known her for years, first as a young sub-lieutenant during his first tour as a commander aboard the USF Centaur. She'd caught his attention then, with her considered decision making, lightning-fast reflexes, and iron will. Later, when he'd risen to the rank of captain on his first ship, the Vulcan, she'd been his senior lieutenant, and he'd noted the changes in her. She'd become a steady and reliable member of the crew, and finally, she'd followed him to the Captivar, a science vessel dedicated to retrieval of those who'd enhance their society with either literature, science, or medical knowledge.

"I may have wanted to be your second, but you didn't tell me I'd have to deal with the sub-minister for retrieval, Alric," Shuran muttered, and she exuded irritation.

"I did warn you that the role wasn't cut-and-dried." Alric smothered the laugh, because Shuran's features had tightened with frustration. "I do understand your concerns, however, it's part of the package, Shuran. Now, I need to go debrief and meet with the medical technicians."

He headed to his office. Once inside he nodded to the technician who would evaluate the information with him.

"I have the results of the first subject. Her health is good, as is nutrition. There is a trace of measles and what they called chicken pox. Apart from that, there's nothing of concern. She'll need a full set of vaccinations."

"You should include the Beta-Gam vaccination too," Alric added.

The technician noted it on the list. "The diagnostic chair detected nothing else of concern. This new generation of diagnostic tools certainly improves on needing to undertake physical scans. Your people did good work there, and I hear they plan to roll them out in medical facilities."

Alric nodded. "Yes. They're working on another, less invasive, bone repair tool currently."

The tech cocked his head. "I'd be interested to know more about that."

Alric shrugged. "I don't know a lot. You know how the scientists are. They keep everything under cover until they are ready to reveal all."

"Sure. Well, that's all I have for you." The tech retreated through the door they'd entered through, and Alric brought up the screen with the results, looking for anomalies.

4

Nala entered the rooms they indicated were to be her private space.

"You have ablution facilities in there, your luggage will be delivered, but should you wish to try current wear, they are in the closet in the corner, and there's a voice-activated screen. It will explain all equipment found in this area." The tiny ID necklace she'd been given hung around her neck, and she stroked it as she listened to the woman who had identified herself as Shuran. "There is a room down the hall which leads to a communal dining and seating area. Educational programming is available on request, both here and there. Simply detach the file unit from your chain and insert it into the reader, if you wish to track your usage."

"When… When will others begin to arrive?" She blinked, because she wasn't sure how much she liked this being the 'first of the cohort' as Shuran had described her.

The woman touched an instrument on her wrist. "We have three beginning to wake, so likely within six hours, I would imagine. Now, I have other tasks to attend, so unless you have queries?"

Nala shook her head. "No. Thank you for your assistance."

The woman stepped back through the door which swooshed shut.

Nala's head was pounding, too much had happened and the way her life had changed. She tottered to the bed and sat down on the edge. "What am I doing here?" she muttered.

"Unable to answer," a voice echoed, and Nala shot up, scanning the room.

"Who's there?"

"This is the voice-activated audio system. Do you have a request?" the voice answered, and as the voice echoed in the room, a subtle shade of purple pulsed through the lighting system.

"Where are you?"

"I am an audio transmission, triggered by your query. My systems are activated by request and generated from a central processing unit within the technical services of the ship. Do you wish to know more?"

Nala opened her mouth. She did but…not now. "Can I ask more questions later on? Do I have to ask them now?"

"All queries, unless they are in violation of the privacy and secrecy codes, may be made at any time."

Well, that answered my questions. "No thank you." Then she realised what she didn't know. "Do you have a name?"

"I am the Voice-Activated Query Unit. Some call me VAQU." The voice pronounced it a Varkku, and Nala nodded.

"Then I will call you VAQU too. Thank you, VAQU."

"You are welcome, designate Nala." The purple ceased and returned to the bright white she was coming to associate with this place.

Nala moved around the room. It was small but contained everything she might require. The wardrobe opened as she touched it, and it produced a suit like that which Shuran wore, and Nala wasn't sure how comfortable she'd be in the clothing.

The bathroom was odd. There was a tube that opened as she approached but no spigot she was used to, and the unit she guessed to be the toilet was strange as well. "How am I supposed to know how to use these?"

"An education program has been designed for designates to explain their use. Would you like me to run that for you on the bedroom screen?" VAQU's voice answered.

"Oh yes, please."

Nala hurried into the bedroom and sat on the end of the bed, watching the program, and though it was brief, it clarified the use of all the equipment. While the toilet was indeed ingenious, it was the sonic shower that was of most interest to her.

She returned to the bathroom, shutting the door, and stripped down, dropping her clothing into the unit she'd been instructed to place them in. Her hair, which she now realised was like a bird's nest of tangles, came next. Nala dug out the pins and popped them on the shelf beside the shower, and strands of hair fell around her face, then she stepped into the tube.

A sensation, like a buzz, fluttered over her body, and she welcomed it. The warmth filled her, and she ran her fingers through her hair, untangling the tresses.

Finally, once the system ceased, she stepped from the unit. "No need for a towel," she mused.

She dragged on the clothing she'd retrieved from the closet, still very much unsure but sighed. It was all she had until either her own things arrived or…

Her stomach rumbled. "Now to find some food," she said.

"Food is available here in your pod, or alternatively in the communal dining area. Would you like to see a menu?" VAQU offered.

"Yes please," she answered.

A slow scrolling list of foods appeared. Most she didn't know, and once more she asked for assistance. In the end, she settled on avian stew, bread rolls, and a fruit platter.

"What drinks are available?" she asked.

"Do you wish alcoholic or non-alcoholic beverages?" VAQU queried.

"Um, tea. A pot of black tea with milk is what I'd like."

The room pulsed in yellow, then VAQU replied, "English black tea, pot, and cup. Milk for serving. Arriving in three minutes."

A small table and chair slid from the wall, and she marvelled again at her surroundings. "Amazing," she muttered and settled herself in time for a small opening to disgorge a tray containing her order.

Alric strode into the communal area three days later, aware that all the new designates were assembled. He'd also called for those crew members who'd be taking on mentorship roles to be present, and they gathered at the end of the room, at parade rest.

"Good morning, everyone. Thank you for coming. As of this morning, all designates will be assigned to their mentors. Mentors, if you could make yourself known to your designates and begin making plans for assisting with housing, educational pursuits, and so on, in a timely manner."

Those sitting at the tables, the designates as they were known, mostly looked vaguely concerned. Within the group there was only one family, consisting of a mother, father, and two young children. They would be assisted by a small team, unlike the others who'd have only a single mentor for their transition.

The archaic constellation aircraft had carried sixty passengers, a crew of five, and five cabin assistants, comprising of a purser, two stewards, and two flight hostesses. That left sixty-six designates to be paired, but over the last few days, they'd all been considered and paired. Arrangements had been made, and some would immediately be embarking on their new lives, while others would disperse in the next day or so.

Alric began working his way through the announcements, explaining the process of mentoring, then matching designates to mentors. It was never easy, this part, and more than once he heard a sharply indrawn breath, or an outpouring of grief that their old life was over.

"Nala Stimson. You will be paired with Captain Alric Reys." He cleared his throat, giving them all just another minute to take in the reality. "I would request that you take this time to meet with your mentor or designate. Fred and Susan Vernis? Please wait as we have arranged a team to work with you, and I will be over soon to explain the situation."

He knew exactly where Nala was sitting, having already spotted her in the group at the table, so he made his way over. She stood and smoothed down the skirt she wore with heavy shoes. "I uh, thank you." She spoke haltingly, and he knew she was controlling the emotions that were no doubt raising hell inside her, because of the slight tremble of her lips.

"It will be alright. But first, I need to talk to the Vernis family. Make sure they understand that the team who will work with them will assemble later today. They will be the first to leave the pods."

She blinked, nodded, and sat back down again, her spine ramrod straight. Something about her actions sat poorly, but he had a task to complete so left her there for the moment.

On the edges of the room sat the small family, and he reasoned that at least they were still whole. The little girl, Emma, shrank back as he approached. "Susan and Fred? I'm sorry you don't have a single mentor to meet right now. We've made arrangements for your family, and that was of our highest priority to ensure you all receive appropriate assistance. We rarely have children aboard the ship, so it was imperative we address their needs."

Fred Vernis was a spare-framed man with glasses obscuring his face, but he stepped in front of his wife and children. "Where are we going?"

"You've been allocated family accommodations on Earth, in what you know as the United States. The children will be enrolled in a special program aiming to bring them up to date with technology and daily life before they can attend an educational facility. You will also attend programs, based on experiences, interests, and life skills applicable to our society," Alric explained.

The man's face turned red. "My wife will stay at home."

Alric shook his head. "She will also be mentored. Should she choose to remain in the home afterward, that is her choice, of course. But she needs to also understand the world she inhabits. You will be moved later today, when the head of the team, Doctor Ren Hesling, arrives."

The man shifted and Alric got the impression that he wasn't happy, but neither were many of the designates he'd worked with—past or present. Alric extended his hand. "Good luck to all of you."

Returning to Nala, Alric was surprised to see the two women she'd been sheltering on the plane huddled together. When they saw him, they sprang apart. "We'll keep in touch, won't we?" the one he knew as Gwendolyn McCarty said, squeezing Nala's hand.

The other, Sarah Levings, squared her shoulders and glared at him. He waited for her to say something, but she simply shook her head, hugged Nala, and stalked away, dragging Gwendolyn off with her.

"Is something wrong?" he asked.

Nala shook her head. "No. We were just working out where we'd be and if it would be possible to keep in touch."

He settled on the seat beside her. "They are all within travelling distance. You'll be in Australia and—" Her sharp inhalation startled him. "What?"

"But... They're being settled in the United States. We won't be able to—"

Alric shook his head. "It's not like you're used to, Nala. For us, getting there is only a matter of four hours travel. And you'll have live, real-time video calling." When she stared at him, he sighed. "You've started your educational programs. One of the early ones talks about communications, yes?"

"Oh, um yes, I think so. But there's so much to take in. I... I forget what they tell you." She clenched a fist, and his first response, the one he had to check, was to cover it with his hand.

"Okay, so audio transmissions are rare these days. Instead, we either use video calling or you can holographically appear too. These are commonplace ways of keeping in contact, irrespective of your location. You could be on Mars and still have that capability."

"Am I likely to end up on Mars?"

He snorted. "Only if you're in trouble. Mars is the penitentiary planet these days. And only for the worst of offenders. It costs too much in shielding to place too many there and to make it habitable for a long-term colony."

"I don't remember…" She glanced down at her now clasped hands. "I have so much to learn, and even knowing where to start seems insurmountable."

"That's what I'm here for," he answered. "Anyway, this is what's going to happen next." He took the next fifteen minutes to explain where she'd be and what opportunities might be open to her. Yet, even as he stood and returned to his office, he had the vague impression that something else was beginning.

Nala waited in the communal dining area at the appointed time of oh-eight-hundred in the morning, her small luggage bag clutched in one hand, handbag in the other.

Gwendolyn rushed up to her. "You're leaving now?"

"It's the time I was given." She bit her lip because the butterflies in her stomach were making her feel nauseated.

Sarah crowded in, the chain she wore around her neck peeking out above the v-neck of her blouse. "I don't like this situation," she growled. "Not one bit. How do we know that things are as they say? This could be a huge conspiracy."

Nala wasn't sure she didn't actually disagree, but the one thing she realised about Sarah after nearly three days of living in close proximity was that she spoke harshly when she was worried. "It'll be fine, Sarah. We'll make the best of it. Isn't that what we all learned during the war?"

Gwendolyn sighed. "It's the war's fault. I wouldn't have been on that plane if I wasn't receiving my husband's medals." In her mid-thirties, Gwendolyn hadn't remarried since the death of her husband, James, in the war. In fact, his file had been sealed, she'd told them, until now. She'd been in Sydney to receive the medals he'd been posthumously awarded.

"You'll take them, the medals, with you?" Nala asked then kicked herself. What else would she do with them? There was no one here who remembered her or her husband, let alone would value them.

"Oh yes." Gwendolyn nodded. "It's all I have. And one photo." The woman's eyes glittered with tears and it gutted Nala.

"We've got each other," she muttered.

Sarah pushed closer, slid one arm over Gwendolyn's shoulder and the other over Nala's. "We're in this together. We're survivors and we'll make a way to stick it out."

Sounds near the entry had Nala looking over her shoulder. The captain had arrived. So she stepped away. "We've got each other's details, and we stay in touch. And I guess, it's time for me to leave, since the captain has arrived."

One last glance at the two women, then Nala turned on the ball of her foot and headed to the doorway.

The captain, Alric as he insisted she call him, waited. He quirked a brow. "Issues?"

Nala shook her head. "No. Just saying goodbye," she explained.

"Alright then. I'll take that," he said and reached for her suitcase.

It wasn't easy to surrender it, given what little she had of her previous life was contained within. "What... How do we get to Earth from here? You said this is a spaceship?"

He laughed. "Yes and no. We're in low orbit around Earth, so we're approximately five hundred and fifteen kilometres above Earth."

Nala stopped in her tracks. "What?" She stared at him.

"About three hundred and twenty miles above Earth. We're sandwiched between two ancient, orbiting objects—an old, deep space telescope and a defunct space station," he explained. "We can't afford to be too far away for the technology to work, because the wormhole technology is limited to less than three hundred and fifty miles. But we keep its capability to around three hundred and eighteen miles as that allows for low-flying craft to be captured. That's around eight thousand feet. Even by your days' piloting standards, that's very low. It was determined to catch aircraft, especially if they are in freefall by the time we locate their signal, with speed."

"I don't understand most of what you just said," she muttered.

"I'll try to explain it to you later. But for now, follow me and we'll board the ship-to-surface craft."

Her stomach wobbled again at the thought of any kind of craft, let alone space travel. This was an idea that was considered fantastical in her own time, yet these people talked about it like it was no more than a walk in the park!

He ushered her towards a long, oblong-looking plane. It had windows just like the plane, except this was covered in a shiny metallic exterior, and was pumping mist through its rear engines. "Is it on fire?" she breathed.

"No. It's merely warming up the engines. The crew have checked it already, and see? Passengers are boarding."

And they were, not that she noted anyone from her group. She felt odd and out of place in her clothing that was so different from anyone else. Most of the women wore the tight pantsuits, with hair that was either short or non-existent in many cases. One woman boarded with purple sparkles in her short coiffure.

He urged her up the four steps and into the cabin. A man waited nearby and held out his hand. "Well, captain, I'll bet your pleased to be on furlough."

Alric grunted. "Yes and no. There's more work to be done to find out what went wrong with the wormhole, but the rules are clear. I must abide by the downtime guidelines. Anyway, seats?"

"Captain Strong thought you'd like the front so you'll get as close to a bird's eye view as possible." They were waved into lounging chairs seated opposite each other with a small table between. "I'll arrange beverages for you once we're underway, but the expected travel time is under an hour today. Once we break through the atmosphere, it seems we've got a pleasant ride, balmy temperatures, and little wind to impede us."

"Excellent," Alric responded, and she waited patiently. "If you'd stow Nala's bag, please?"

"Of course," the man said and retrieved it from Alric. When the man glanced to Nala, he smiled. "You're a new designate, I understand. You may prefer the rear-facing seat in that case." He pointed to one and she settled herself in.

"Thanks, Nico. I'll take it from here," Alric added, and the man bowed and left them to it.

"I'll help you with the harness." He reached over and pulled the straps up so they covered her shoulders and met on her lap. "There," he said. "Safe and sound."

Nala wasn't sure she could trust her voice. Right now, it took every ounce to appear calm and keep the screams from erupting. She nodded her thanks, clasped her hands together, and silently prayed they'd arrive at their destination in one piece.

Alric could see how terrified she was, the clasped hands and her pallor were big giveaways. "It's okay, Nala. We aren't going to crash."

She closed her eyes and he cursed himself internally, realising the insensitivity of his comment.

"Damn. I'm sorry, Nala. I didn't think."

She opened her eyes. "It's okay. I mean, you've done this how many times?"

"Hundreds, I'd guess."

She covered her eyes for a moment as the engines rumbled. "I should be stronger," she murmured. "You've done this before. That was only my fourth flight ever, and I was heading home."

"Where were you coming back from?" It might be best if she talked, he thought. Keep her mind active and engaged so she didn't dwell on the travel.

"I was attending a conference in France, discussing the principles and practices of nursing education. We were flying into Brisbane." She shook, but forced her hands away from her eyes and into her lap, then stared at him. "It was a great honour to be part of the Australian contingent. I stayed back several days though, because my cousins were meeting me there from England. It's why I didn't come back with the other ladies."

"Your family were English?" He frowned. "But aren't you Australian?"

Nala smiled. "Yes and no. My sister, Veronica, and I were born in England, and we emigrated after the war in forty-six. Edmund was born about a month after we arrived in Australia. We consider ourselves Australian though."

He gave a small, surprised laugh. "So, then you became a nurse. That would have been very interesting."

She sighed. "I wanted to be a doctor, but Mother and Father told me that it wouldn't be right. There were boys who'd gone to war and had missed out on their chance. That they should... They were entitled to the placement, and as a female, I should be satisfied. My parents wanted me to marry and settle down, like Veronica." She shrugged. "I guess it probably seems strange to you, but they had to agree for me to apply. And they didn't, so the next closest option was to become a nurse. So, I did."

"That doesn't sound right." It puzzled him that her parents wouldn't support her decision. "I mean, you wanted... You had good enough educational output?"

She frowned. "Educational output?"

"You did well in your schooling."

"Oh, grades," she muttered. "Yes. I was an honours student."

"That meant you could access any course?" he asked.

"With their permission, yes. It's how things work in our time. Can the girls in your time make any decision they want without needing to ask for permission?"

"Of course they can. I mean, obviously there are some caveats around that. You can't pair up... Er, marry under age, and there are some things that affect community and or safety of civilians. Things like that," he answered.

She rubbed a spot between her eyes.

"You have a headache?"

"Yes. No. I'm confused," she whispered. "It doesn't make sense that a woman can make those decisions without needing to seek parental input."

"Would you have chosen to go against their decision if things had been different?"

Before she could respond, Nico arrived to take their drink order. Alric waited as Nala requested a juice after listening to the options. He ordered a coffee and watched as Nico arranged their drinks, then served them. Then once again alone, he lifted his cup to his mouth, waiting for her to consider the question.

She seemed to ponder as she sipped her drink, eyes downcast, hands shaking. "I... I don't know. I'd like to say yes, but I don't know." She lifted her gaze to him. "Is it too late to find out more?"

Alric considered her near inaudible query. "No, but we would need to consider how this may be achieved."

"You don't think I could, do it? Become a doctor?"

He shook his head. "Not necessarily, but it will depend on placements, bridging courses and so on. Let's find out before any further decisions are made."

"Of course," she whispered again and sipped at her drink.

The flight continued, but it was clear Nala's attention was full of considering her future and her past. He realised that requiring her to give up her entire life meant a total change in her. He'd never been paired with a designate, so he hadn't understood the level of loss they experienced. It was unnerving to see up close how they looked to overcome not just loss of their lives, but also identity.

Previously Nala had been a daughter, a student, a sister. She'd been a nurse and obviously a good one if they'd sent her to France to discuss training other nurses. The world she knew had changed, and all that was left was a tenuous connection through others who'd been aboard the plane and her tiny suitcase and handbag.

How could that be enough to sustain her through her life?

It made him question the ethics of pulling people from their pre-destined futures and playing God. Were they right to do this? How did someone overcome such loss?

When the landing announcement was made, he pulled himself together and reached for her hand. "Nala, hold on if you'd like."

She reached out, took his hand, and squeezed as the land rose toward them. "Thank you," she muttered as the craft touched gently down on the runway.

Once they'd docked, he unclipped himself and assisted her, and they rose. Nico was there with her battered suitcase, and they stepped through the doors of the craft.

Hustle and bustle heralded her new life as people scurried around. Announcements blared on the loudspeaker, and she huddled close to him.

"This way," he instructed, and they moved toward the baggage lift. He took control of his bag and ushered her to the front.

"Is it… Is everything like this?"

He laughed. "No. This is a busy day. But come, we'll be met at the front. I organised transport for us."

They exited the building and there, waiting, was a small, white aircar, and he urged her forward. "Hop in and I'll stow our bags," he said, taking hers from her grasp again.

Nala's first thoughts were 'there's so many people' followed by 'how am I going to learn to navigate in this world' as she watched the sea of people entering and exiting the silver and glass building.

Inside the car was like being in a cocoon, and she wondered if she could stay there, safe.

Alric climbed inside. "Come on, seatbelt." As he had on the shuttle, Alric made sure to snap the two pieces together then settled to his.

Once again Nala looked down. "We didn't have these. In our time, I mean."

Will I ever get used to talking about my life in past tense? Tears scorched inside her eyelids, and she closed them. What choice do I have? If my old life is gone…?

She gripped the handles of her bag tight. Her mother had made it for her when she'd announced she'd been chosen to travel to France. She'd said any daughter of hers travelling to a place where fashion was created needed to be outfitted accordingly. Her bag held the entirety of her new wardrobe, containing a new evening gown, three skirts, and five blouses. It had been the height of fashion then, but now? It was ancient and out of place. Out of time.

He took her hand again, and she sighed. *He must think I'm a watering pot.* She wasn't. Not really. But the shocks of the last week had forced her into an unknown world and time. One where she had no power to determine who and what she was. She was simply a designate.

The internal thoughts forced her to straighten up. It was time to stop wallowing in her loss and find a way to grapple with her new reality. *Is that what I've been doing these last few days?* "Oh yes, my girl."

"Did you say something?" Alric enquired.

She laughed. "I'm telling myself to straighten up. I can't… Wallowing isn't like me. I didn't despair after my parents made their decision, and I'm not going to start now."

"Oh." He looked surprised at her announcement.

Looking out the window, she considered what she knew. She couldn't go home. She had to build a new life, and while she had regrets, she could make the best of it. Take the chance that had been denied to her.

Biting her lip, she realised that she only had her memory to rely on to remember what her family looked like. "Is there some way to find photos of my parents? To learn what happened to my siblings?"

He started at her question. "I don't know. We could make enquiries of the museum, as they've retrieved records. We do have a list of lost planes and those aboard. Perhaps they kept details of families too?"

She nodded. "That's good. A place to start." She sat back in her chair and looked forward. "How long until we reach my home?"

"Ours," he corrected.

"What?" The word surprised her. "Ours? How do you mean?"

"Designates are usually housed either with their mentors for the first period or close by, depending on housing stocks. In my case, I have a house, which is quite unusual, but I inherited it from my family. I have ample room for you. You just need to watch out for Sunny."

"Sunny? Is that your dog?"

He laughed, and crinkles appeared at the sides of his eyes. "Oh, she'd love to hear that. No. Sunny is…" His laughter died away. "She's my half-sister. She lives in my home while I'm away, and I asked her to stay for a little longer. Just until you're acclimated. She can help you with things I…" He shrugged. "Female things, I guess. Normally designates get a same-sex placement. You didn't because we try to find a leader in each crew we retrieve, and you were it. Leaders are placed with senior officers, and I was the only one available this time around. Normally it would have been Shuran, but she's just taken on the role as my second and is… She's not in a position at this time to take on a designate."

"Oh." Nala didn't understand his hesitation, but she accepted it. "Well, that should be fine as we have a chaperone."

He quirked a brow at her. "Chaperone?"

"Yes. Oh, you don't have them in your time?" She stared at him.

"No."

"Then how do you court?"

5

lric couldn't help but explode with laughter. "Court? I'm guessing you meant date. Women, men, and all the variants in between set their own rules and standards. In fact, I've never heard of a chaperone."

He watched as Nala straightened up. "If a woman wishes to keep her virtue unquestioned, she'd have a chaperone. Even in the nurses' home, if we were out with any man, we were required to have someone with us. Another woman."

"It seems to me there were a lot of rules around your daily life. Anyway, here we are. This is my home." The vehicle pulled up beside his house. If he considered it, based on images he'd seen in history classes, he might call it a boxy structure, with glass shimmering in the daylight.

"It's… It's different," she breathed.

He withheld the laughter. "Come on. Sunny is waiting for us."

Alric showed her the button to press to remove the seatbelt, then assisted her from the vehicle. She waited as he grabbed their bags then shadowed him up the small walkway.

"You have some land?" she asked.

He shook his head. "Land is at a premium. Houses like this are also rare. This one was built about three hundred years ago, and to be honest, Sunny keeps telling me it's hard work to keep habitable. We've retrofitted as much as possible, but some aspects are impossible to replace, especially since they designated it as a historical artifact."

She opened her mouth as if to argue and he wondered if she was going to tell him she knew what he meant. But of course, they weren't building houses like this when she lived in the past.

"Come on in," he said.

He ushered her into a hallway, and she glanced up. "So much light," she enthused, and he couldn't help but smile as he placed the luggage on the floor. She added her handbag at the same time.

Noise echoed down the hallway, and before he could say anything else, a zoom of energetic female launched into his arms. "Alric! Finally. I've got all kinds of surprises." Sunny was in her early twenties and a student of archaeology, which she said was why she simply adored his home. In her signature whirling, dervish activity, she squirmed until he freed her from his hug. "And you must be Nala. It's so great to have you here. Alric says I'm not supposed to pester you, and to let you settle, but my university crew and I have a debate on early twentieth century lifestyles..."

"Not now, Sunny. We've just arrived, and a coffee or tea would be welcome."

Sunny pouted as she was wont to, but she retreated to the kitchen zone. "Fine. But I get to ask questions later," she called out.

Alric turned to Nala. "Sorry about that. She's the baby and indulged by her parents."

Nala stared at him. "She's your half-sister but she's... Is she Asian?"

It took a moment for Alric to understand the question. "Chinese. My stepmother is Chinese, but you might need to be careful asking questions like that. No one much cares about the culture, it's what's beneath the surface."

Nala blushed deeply. "I apologise if I offended," she said quietly.

He breathed out, realising that indeed the difference in time meant that the language and appropriate behaviour were significantly changed. He'd been warned this was the case, but still… "You didn't offend, and I doubt Sunny will be either, but others can get upset. Society has changed and—"

"There was an educational program about changes to society that I haven't yet viewed. I will, of course, make that a priority if there is a screen in—"

"Yes, there is a screen in your room. Look Nala, I want to help you," he said, feeling helpless, because she was stiff and formal now. He reached for her, but she shook her head, not encouraging the connection.

"It's fine. I have a lot to learn, but I'm quick, captain. I'll make a short study of it and begin to seek my own accommodations as soon as possible." The white bracketing the sides of her mouth betrayed just how deeply she felt his words and he cursed himself again.

Sunny came dashing back into the room. "Well now, I have coffee for Alric and I and tea for you. I wasn't sure—" She stopped talking, clearly picking up on the tension in the air.

"I'd love that cup of tea," Nala said and reached for the cup. "Do you have milk?"

"Oh, I was about to ask," Sunny said, before shooting a 'what's going on' look at Alric.

"Thanks, Sunny. Let's go to the lounge," he said and steered Nala towards the room at the front.

She perched on the edge of a chair, like it was going to bite her.

"Aren't these chairs cool?" Sunny said. "I found them in an old antique store. They said there were over two hundred years old. Did you have seats like this?"

Nala smiled tightly. "No. Our seats were more… utilitarian, I guess. But if you've got some things you'd like to ask me, I'm more than willing."

Sunny grinned, but Alric caught the slight frustration that tinged Nala's words.

Sunny was bubbly and effervescent, but Nala was struggling to hold her equilibrium. For some reason, it was fine for Alric's sister to ask questions about inanities, yet when she too had questions, they were somehow out of line. Things had changed, but that much? She didn't seethe so much as feel there was some kind of imbalance.

Nala sighed in her mind. She had so much to learn, and clearly what was and wasn't okay to discuss remained high on that list.

"So, you were born before the first space expedition and well before the uprising of 2085 where the first moon-base mission was almost compromised. How exciting is it that you ended up in space through a wormhole, which captured your plane before it crashed?"

Nala felt a bubble of panic rising in her chest and raised her hand. Nearly crashed, in space, and wormhole. Nausea raised its head.

Alric moved, grabbing her hand. "Not now, Sunny."

Nala clawed at his hand.

"It's okay. Just breathe." From his pocket, he grabbed a mask and handed it to her. "Use this to help even out your breathing."

Closing her eyes, she followed his instructions, and listened to his steady cadence.

"That's right. In and out. Take your time. You're safe," Alric soothed.

Once she finally had her breath back, she glanced at Sunny, who sat, wide eyes, watching, tears filling her eyes. "I'm so sorry. I didn't realise."

Shaking her head, Nala inhaled. "It's okay. I'm just... It's a topic I have some issues in right now. But if you wouldn't mind, I think I'd like to lie down?"

Alric reached for her hand. "I'll show you to your rooms. You have a private bathing room, as you're in the guest rooms."

"Thank you. But I need to look for somewhere..." Nala shut up, because the look he aimed at her was piercing.

"I know Sunny upset you, and so did I. I didn't realise the enormity of what we asked of you, but I want to help you. That means you need to work with me, to learn how to survive in this world."

Right now, all Nala wanted was to survive. And he was right that she needed to learn how to do that. She needed his assistance, but that didn't mean she had to like it, or just be buffeted by what had happened. He'd already told her that women of this time were empowered. That they could and did make their own decisions, and in that moment, she decided that was what she'd do. She'd be strong, in control of her destiny. It just meant relying on him for a little while to achieve that outcome.

Nala straightened her shoulders. "You're right. I need to learn how to survive, so I'll stay here. Learn what I need to know, and one day, I'll walk out that door."

When he frowned, she hid a smile. "You don't have to rush…" He placed her suitcase and handbag inside the room he'd directed her to, and reached out.

Nala evaded the gesture. "I'd really like to take a nap, and shower. Then I think I'll watch a couple of programs."

He bowed a little from the waist. "Of course. As you require. Dinner will be at seventeen hundred hours. We keep reasonably early hours here, so I'll see you then."

She waited for him to leave, then settled on the bed. "Well, I guess a shower then those programs." The thing was, she just couldn't summon up the energy to rise. Out of time and out of place, she was exhausted by the trauma of the day. The day was not even half over, and she was ready to collapse. "But I can't." There was too much to do, and learn. She had decisions to make and a life to build. Restarting her life in her mid-twenties felt like a mountain she needed to overcome.

Her hand twitched, and she wished there was a pad and a pencil to make a list. Her hand strayed to the handbag, then dove inside. She found a scrap of paper, and the stub of a pencil. The one she always carried in her bag.

Placing the paper on her knee, Nala bit her lip. "Where do I start?"

Under normal circumstances, she'd understand the world she was in.

Watch as many programs on social customs as possible.

In her mind this was key, because missteps would be unwelcome.

People may be somewhat understanding in the future, but she couldn't rely on it.

Find employment.

That would allow the next item she etched on the list.

Find somewhere to live.

Buy a wardrobe that's acceptable to now.

All key aspects to fitting in.

Now that she had the start of a list, she felt a little more empowered. Stronger. More able to survive this new world.

"Shower now," she told herself and considered the room. It was comfortable, though not quite what she was used to in a guest room. "Things are different. I need to learn to cope."

6

Alric sat at the dining table. Sunny had finally left to attend her classes, and honestly, he was grateful. He loved his sister. Usually, she was the best company to have around. Just, not today.

He was brooding. It wasn't a useful emotion, but something about the situation with Nala blurred the edges of his mind. He'd accepted that she had a lot to learn, and would need assistance, yet she didn't want that. What did that say about him? That he wanted her to rely on his help was a failing he didn't want to accept.

He stood and pushed his cup into the recess, so the auto-clean unit would prepare it for use next time.

Glancing out the window, he pondered, for the first time, what this area would have looked like three hundred, or even seven hundred, years ago. The windows were fully connected to a video emitter, and in a split-second decision he stood and grabbed his communications device, which had an application to change the scenery. He scanned through and found vision of the past.

He wondered what she'd think about this, making the change so she'd be more comfortable. So he could understand what she'd lost.

He considered his communications device once more. "Show me any records relating to the loss of a super constellation in 1956."

There were two listings, and he realised neither of them was her plane and cursed. The communication device would only undertake a cursory search, unless he ordered otherwise. His family had long ago disabled the system routines allowing a deep research sweep on a single enquiry.

"How did they manage to lose multiple planes?" But the truth was, according to history, this kind of travel was still largely experimental by the standards of today. He didn't read more, because they wouldn't offer a scrap of information concerning what happened to her family.

He grunted and stalked into the area he called his office. Once, it had been the master suite of the house, but he'd connected the technology that allowed him to work and study remotely, depending on the circumstances. Settling in his pod chair, he sighed as the room glowed with a subtle white that reminded him he was fully connected once more.

"VAQU? Can you find me any records for the super constellation lost in March 1956? I'm looking for details of families left behind."

"Working on it, Alric." The room glowed with a tinge of purple during the communications, and it calmed the nerves that gnawed at him. "I have detected two forms of records. One pertains to a compensation listing all contacts for those lost aboard the super constellation returning to Brisbane from Sydney. The other concerns the search for the plane. Which do you wish to see?"

"Both."

The holographic representations of the documents flashed up, and he looked at the information, scanned it. The flight had downed while over the ocean, avoiding bad weather on a direct flight. The weather had whipped up, and a tornado had been sighted.

No wreckage or bodies had ever been located. "That's because we plucked them out of the sky." But in truth, he wondered if the tornado had been a result of the wormhole. "Anything's possible." He tapped a note onto the desk screen, reminding himself to consider that they may have been responsible for the crash. If that was so… How many other craft losses had they initiated?

The thought nauseated him, but he was committed to this path now, so with a swipe of his hand, he dismissed the findings and scanned the list of compensation payments.

"Nala Stimson. Nurse. Aged twenty-four. Compensation payment of five thousand pounds sterling was made to her parents, based on her wages and equivalent to a six-year payout." He pondered that. Six years' worth of wages to compensate her family for such a loss. "So little."

He added the names of her parents, seeking information as to what had become of them. Of her father there were snippets here and there. He'd been a highly decorated soldier in the English army during the war. They'd emigrated and he'd lived to the ripe old age—for then—of eighty. A funeral notice had been posted of her mother who'd passed some three years after the plane loss.

"VAQU, print this information for me."

"Print, Alric?"

He grunted. Printing was only endorsed in certain circumstances. Due to a range of environmental factors, it was considered only for serious situations such as major government events, in hospitals for the transportation of those unable to communicate and those deceased. And by those who were working with designates from the pre-printing-prohibition era.

"Verification of reason required," VAQU intoned.

"Information required by designate to learn what happened to her family," he answered.

The room glowed blue. "Working," VAQU confirmed.

He waited. Nothing could occur until assent was granted by the print prohibition office.

"Authorisation granted," VAQU offered several minutes later.

The chatter of printing made a ka-chunk ka-chunk noise, and though it was invasive, he ignored the irritation. He knew this was one piece of information he could give Nala.

"VAQU, find all information concerning her family, siblings, and nephews and nieces. Send a report to my comms device."

"Acknowledged," came the reply.

Nala's stomach rumbled, and she glanced away from the screen, looking for the digital clock. Four-forty. Alric had mentioned dinner would be around seventeen hundred hours. She was used to the twenty-four-hour clock with her nursing duties, living with an ex-soldier father, and of course the war. All these had impressed on her the need for promptness. So, she stilled the program and stood up.

Looking down at herself, she sighed, taking in the clunky shoes, the dun-brown A-line skirt with a central pleat, and the khaki green shirt, which she knew was considered medieval by the standards of the world she inhabited.

"I'm going to have to buy new clothes," she said aloud.

Sunny had been dressed in bright colours; a suit so tight it outlined every aspect of her body. Nala couldn't dress like that but would need assistance. She knew Alric had said Sunny would assist with female aspects, but she realised that he was the best chance she had for choosing something a little less outrageous.

Making her way through the house, she accepted that she'd need money, or credits, as the previous program had informed her. There were still two more designate-specific tutorials to be viewed, but she'd started to get a handle on the realities of this new world.

Alric was hovering, and when she entered the room, he smiled. "Come. Sit down. I've made a meal which I think should entice you. It's not really from your time, but as close as I could find. I hope you find it to be satisfactory."

The scent of meat filled the air, and she inhaled deeply. "It smells good," she offered, though she kept a distance between them. Self-preservation, she told herself as she settled in one of the chairs he indicated. She'd have to learn to live her life without others. She needed to protect herself now.

He grabbed two plates from the food energiser. "This is called lamb goulash. I don't know if you've had it before?"

"Goulash? Hmm, I think so. Some of the ladies in the camp were from Hungary, and sometimes they'd have a meal where everyone brought a plate," she said.

"Camp?" He blinked. "I don't know what that is."

It was difficult trying to work out how to explain the nuances of her life before, she thought. "When we emigrated, got off the boat, we went to big camps. Thousands of people lived there. The site used to be army barracks during the war, and I guess it made sense to put everyone in there. It's where new immigrants started until they could find a home. So, a bit of a mix of nationalities. Anyway, there were some Hungarian families, and I kind of vaguely remember having a hot dish like this." She pointed to the meal on her plate.

"It must have been scary," he said, sitting opposite her. "A new country and people you don't know."

Thoughts cascaded and she swallowed the lump lodged in her throat. "It was different. We'd been on the ship for weeks, and I guess we had a kind of community. Then it grew when we arrived. It was good though. Australia was great. Welcoming. So many opportunities, which was why Mum and Dad brought us there. Veronica met Fred there. Her husband. She was only thirteen when we arrived, and Fred was two years older, and they were inseparable." She shrugged.

"You were close?" he asked, and she sighed.

"Not really. Veronica was a girly girl. For her it was all about skirts and dancing. Once she and Fred became a pair, there was nothing else as far as she was concerned. She found a job at the local supermarket and worked there until they married. She said a girl had to save for her glory box, and she wanted to be ready when the time came."

"I'm sorry you had to leave them behind," he said, and she could hear the sincerity in his words.

Tears burned. "I've learned to remake my life before. I can do it again," she whispered. But it did hurt. There was no anchor. No one to confide in.

"I found some things I think you may find interesting. After the plane disappeared, your parents received a compensation payment." He pushed a small pile of pages toward her.

"Really?" She glanced down at them. Scanned. "Five thousand pounds?"

"Was that a lot?"

She nodded. "Yes. I…"

"I'm…" He shifted in his seat. "I've set VAQU to search for more information for you. I guess it's the least we can do. Maybe we'll find some photos too. I thought you'd like that."

Now the tears streamed down her face, and she hunted for the handkerchief she'd stashed in her pocket. Memories of her grandmother always reminding her that a lady had one on hand. Another thing lost and she felt so alone.

She wiped away the tears, aware he was watching. Probably feeling helpless, she guessed.

"I'm so sorry, Nala. I didn't mean to upset you."

She stuffed the handkerchief back in her pocket. "No. What you did was very kind and thoughtful, and I appreciate it." She reached over the table to take his hand. "Thank you, Alric." She sighed heavily. "And we should eat this excellent meal you've cooked," she said. Hoping the change of subject would help her regain her equilibrium.

They ate quietly with only the odd interruption. Nala enquired where Sunny was, and Alric replied, "She's in school, she had a lecture this evening."

"Ah," Nala muttered. "She's only here at some parts of the day?"

"Only for another week, then she's heading home to her mother's house. Our father died three years ago, and that's when I inherited this place. We lived here for a few years after my grandparents died, then when Sunny was born, Linn wanted to be closer to her parents. So, they moved to Perth, and now Sunny commutes, attending monthly face-to-face and activity events, but her book work is completed at home."

"So, how old is she?"

"Sunny is nearly twenty-three. Before she started to stay here, a distant cousin would house-sit for me. But she's now working on a craft out of the Orion Quadrant. So, Sunny stepped up, but it's only a couple of times a year so…" He shrugged.

Nala gazed at him. "Don't you ever get lonely?" Then she paled. "I shouldn't pry. Forgive me."

He laughed gently. "It's not prying. And no, not really. I've got my crew and friends from the academy. I've got Linn and Sunny. I lead a fulfilled life."

"But you're not married."

He considered the words and knew it was necessary to explain. "No. I nearly did once, years ago. It didn't work out, and I'm pleased, really. Halle was great, but she's now a captain in her own right and runs regular shuttles for the penitentiary on Mars. If we'd still been together, I'm not sure we would have lasted much longer. We both had plans and that's what ultimately told us we didn't belong together. I wanted science and exploration and a command. She wanted her own command with regular hours and services. We're… I guess, we're better friends than anything else."

He watched as Nala bit her lip.

"You weren't married either," he pointed out.

She laughed, but there was little mirth in it. "No. If I married, I'd have to give up nursing. I never met a man who made me desire that outcome. I didn't want to be like Veronica or my mother. Even that family, you know, Susan Vernis who'd been on the plane with me? She'd obviously been content with her children and husband."

"Things aren't like that anymore."

She blinked. "Pardon?"

"If you decide to return to nursing or become a doctor, you don't have to give up anything when you marry. The choice to marry, as old-fashioned as it is, isn't an ending of an occupation, calling, or role."

She picked up her spoon, which she'd laid down when asking about Sunny, and tasted the food again. He knew she was looking for time to think and consider, so he followed suit and waited.

Moments stretched out as they ate, and when her bowl was empty, she pushed it away. "I've been watching the programming for designates. I need to find out how to undertake the required bridging training, find a place of my own, and learn how to earn credits."

"You've time for the housing, and in fact, you can stay here for a while, so you don't need to worry about housing. And when the time comes, I'll help you." He didn't miss the mulish look on her face at his words and held up a hand before she could interrupt. "Hear me out. Applying for housing is dependent on your role, so until we get you through the bridging course, it's better if you stay here. In terms of credits, we'll take you to a government identification centre tomorrow and enrol you, complete the paperwork for you to apply for a learn-to-drive permit and open a crediting account."

"That's all wonderful, but I need clothes and—"

"When we open your crediting account, there is an ex-gratia payment made. Given all the changes you need to make, it's usually sufficient to see you set up for at least a year. It can be used for clothing, housing, and food. There are other grants and benefits made available, and we'll talk about that tomorrow."

She sighed, and a beep indicated an incoming communication. He looked down and swore.

"What's wrong?" Nala asked.

"There's been an accident. One of your fellow designates has been admitted to the high-care medical unit."

She paled. "Who?"

"A Maxwell Grimes," Alric answered. "Do you... Do you know him?"

Nala shook her head. "No. Not really. I mean we introduced each other, but he was one of those I met and didn't really commit to memory. Will he be alright?"

"I don't know," Alric said.

He pondered the communication. It was odd; usually designates spent the first few days quietly, so to be injured was... strange.

He put the thought away for now. "What are your plans for this evening?"

"I didn't rest this afternoon, so I think once we clean up, I should head to bed. If you don't mind, of course."

"The auto-clean unit will take care of most of it. We just need to lodge the plates and cups and it does the rest."

She frowned. "So, no washing up? Hmm, I think I could like that. I'd also like a look at the laundry facilities and… How did you cook today's dinner? I don't see an oven or stove."

He laughed. "There's a cooking recess for those things, but usually, most people purchase pre-prepared meals and load the auto-cook unit."

"Auto-cook unit?"

He smiled. "I'll show you tomorrow. We do have one, I just prefer not to use it."

7

Alric rose bright and early. Today he was going to escort Nala to the identification unit and start her on the path to her future. At the edge of his mind was the knowledge that she'd have a future where she was in control. One where she'd hopefully meet someone. Forge a life.

"Get out of your head, Alric."

He rose, bathed then dressed. In the kitchen, Nala was already waiting, a cup of tea in her hand. "Oh, I hope you don't mind. I had Sunny show me how to order drinks. Would you like a coffee?"

He grinned. "I'd love that, thanks."

She made the request then waited for his coffee to be disgorged.

As she handed it to him, he accepted the cup with a "thank you." He sipped the coffee and felt the burn of the warm liquid in his throat. It was welcome as the day was cooler than he'd experienced on Earth for a while, not to mention the temperature-controlled environment on board his ship.

She smiled at him. "What time do you wish to leave?"

"I'd like to leave within the hour. If you have any certification or identification on you, please bring that with you. I have the necessary documentation for the unit so that they have the details of your arrival."

She nodded. "Of course. Uh, Sunny also asked me to alert you to the fact that she leaves on Monday. She wanted to know if I wanted to visit the mercantile to purchase clothing. I told her I'd need to know what you have planned in the next few days."

He nodded. "We could stop by the mercantile tomorrow if that suits her. It might be worthwhile if I come with you. Unless you don't want me there?"

Nala's eyes widened. "Oh, I think I'd prefer you there. I'm... I don't know what's appropriate and suitable for whatever meetings or events I may be likely to attend."

"Fine then. We'll visit the mercantile tomorrow. I'll send Sunny a message." Mind you, he didn't know why Sunny hadn't just sent the message directly to him in the first place, rather than sending it circuitously through Nala.

Nala followed Alric into the large, white building. There were lines hovering around what she now understood to be input units—non human interfaces which dealt with a range of basic issues.

"So, what happens if the input units can't fix the issue?" Nala queried.

"Well, you'll find out in a moment." He steered her toward a line which was signed 'birth and alien registration.' They stepped within the cordoned-off area and followed those in the line before them until they reached the input unit.

A screen showed a message. 'Birth registration or alien?' Two buttons lit up on the screen, and he depressed the one labelled alien.

'More data required, await a technician.'

A gateway opened and Alric ushered her through. "Now what?" she questioned, and he smiled.

"We take a seat and wait for a technician. Over here," he said and found her an empty chair in the area assigned 'waiting area.'

He settled in the seat beside her, but within minutes a man came up to them. "Alien registration?"

Alric extended the sheaf of papers in his hand. "We have a designate registration."

The man's eyes gleamed. "Then come this way."

Alric didn't miss that Nala stuck close to him, and when they settled in one of the privacy cubicles, her chair slid as close to his as possible without being too obvious. He placed a hand on her knee after noting she was starting to bounce it up and down, probably with nerves.

"I'm Captain Alric Reys of the Captivar. This is my designate, Nala Stimson." He slid the papers onto the desk and waited for the man to scan them.

"Ah. Yes. I need a specialist then for this. One moment." The man rose and scurried from the cubicle.

"You can remove your hand," Nala said in a tight voice.

He dragged it away as if scalded. "Pardon me. I thought you might need some assurance."

She sighed. "I'm really out of my depth in this situation. I'm just a girl from so long ago, and I have no understanding of the rules or how to do this, but I still have control of my faculties and don't need you placing your hand in an area I consider to be inappropriate." She blushed a deep red.

"I didn't mean to embarrass you," he said. He'd simply sought to give her the support he thought she'd need.

"I'm overreacting probably. I know you don't mean anything by it, but in my time..." Her words were near whisper and it shamed him that she felt so uncomfortable with his support.

Alric shook his head. "It's not appropriate here either. I forgot myself."

When she exhaled and nodded, he breathed a sigh of relief, and was pleased when a woman slid into the booth.

"Well now, Captain Reys and Ms Stimson. Johly has explained the situation to me." She waved the papers in the air. "Let's get this paperwork started, shall we?"

She took relevant information, accessed the central databank of details collated during Nala's time on the Captivar, and finally, a specialised printer in the corner—one registered to the office he surmised—spat out an official identification chip.

"Ms Stimson, as is required by the law of Earth, you must carry this registration chip with you at all times. Should the chip be requested by duly recognised officials of the law enforcement fraternity, you are required to make it available for scanning."

"Thank you," Nala responded.

The tiny metal chip was slid across the desk, then the woman left them in the cubicle, and Alric understood that was to give them a minute or two for him to assist her in arranging a secure location to place it.

Alric reached into his pants pocket. "I have this. A lot of women wear it as a charm on a bracelet. Sunny had a spare and thought you may wish to have it."

He picked up the chip and sat it inside a clasped retainer on the chain and handed it over. She took it and fumbled with the clasp. "Would you help me, please?" she whispered, and he reached over to assist.

There was something incredibly intimate about the action and how close he was to her, and his body reacted, tightened. Straightening up, he noted the fineness of her features. The brown eyes so deep they were like the depths of space, and the length of her lashes. The scent of her, womanly.

He tugged back but not before he noticed the way her eyes darted to his. The alarm present in the quickness of her breathing.

Not good, he told himself. He couldn't let any kind of emotional attachment get in the way of his role as her mentor.

Nala glanced away, and he cleared his throat. "We should be heading out. There's still more to do today."

Nala brushed at her skirt as the woman re-entered the cubicle. "All done then? Right, I'll see you out."

They rose and together headed to the front of the building, but just before they left, the woman called, "Wait! I meant to give you this. It's the log-in to Nala's account. An initial grant of forty thousand credits has been deposited. Once the log-in requirements have been completed, and an official contact account is enacted, a further grant will be allocated."

A small chip was thrust at him, and he took it. "Thank you," he said and ushered Nala from the building.

"What's...?" Nala asked.

"Let's go get some refreshments and I'll explain it all," he told her.

Nala settled into the seat while Alric placed the order on the holo-menu.

She fingered her bracelet, the one he'd placed on her wrist, and waited for him to settle on refreshments. Yet another frustration in a world of them for her. Including that interlude in the office just earlier.

"So, what is this about a log-in requirement?" she queried, thinking she should find out how things worked rather than focusing on his confidence and good looks. After all, good looks meant nothing if the man was a cad.

"The log-in requirements are arranging an account that you can self-service..." He likely saw the lack of understanding on her face, because he cleared his throat. "You've seen my communications device," he said and waved it in front of her. "We use these to connect with each other, to check things, and to send messages. Well, in this case, they also allow us to interact with various aspects of government. We need to collect a device for you, then we create an account that you can check. The chip we were given at the end? That is like access to credit. While you have your identichip in the bracelet, this one allows you to make purchases."

A beep heralded the delivery of drinks, and she accepted hers from the strange-looking waiter, then sipped. "This is nice," she murmured.

"It's raspberry and black tea. You told me you like raspberries in the initial interview. Back on the Captivar."

His words were a jolt. He remembered something she'd said in conversation like that? "I..." She shook her head, because she couldn't afford to be sidetracked, not when she was aware her situation was unsettled.

"Once we have you set up, we can see the guidelines of the initial grant they've made. That will allow us to make some decisions about what next. In the short term, our focus is to get your registrations in order, to focus on your education and—"

His communications device heralded another incoming message, and he looked down, while she waited.

"What...?" There was shock in his voice, and she leaned forward.

"Is everything alright? Is it Sunny?"

Alric shook his head. "There's been another accident. Another of your friends... They think he's been poisoned." He raised his eyes to her. "Something is very wrong with this situation."

Her gut clenched. "Who?"

"A James McLean," he answered.

In her mind, she conjured up the vision of a tall, blonde-haired and blue-eyed man. Australian born with the lean physique of someone who worked in the bush. He'd been off a sheep station, she remembered.

"He's a nice man," she muttered. "What makes them think it may be poison?"

"I would imagine a toxicology test. They're almost instantaneous so..." He shrugged.

"This all seems strange. Two of the men are in hospital..." She had a sudden thought. "Will he survive?"

"The authorities seem to think so. It's a common household substance, and he was found quickly." His gaze narrowed. "He'd just arrived on a ship with several others from the Captivar."

"Perhaps he made a mistake," she said, but to be honest, they had all been careful of any substance, since they didn't really know what was okay. Unless it came from the food portal, no one had been game to try anything. Not that this knowledge really settled her nerves, which quivered and jumped.

"So, we need to head to the communications centre to find a device for you."

"I don't have any money… credits," she corrected.

"Remember? You do. The second chip will be implanted in your device once we choose it. That is your access to funds." Alric smiled. "Once you get the hang of it, it's all fairly simple."

She frowned. "What do people do without a device?"

Now, Alric's frown was deep. "Only those without a home are without a device. The device is registered to your home—"

She raised her hand, cutting him off. "If it's registered to your home, then how do I register mine?"

He laughed, and in her belly, something squishy and warm moved. "We register it to my home address, then when you find your own home, we transfer that registration."

Opening her mouth, then closing it again was all Nala could manage for long seconds.

"Nala? It's really quite simple."

Transfer. Own home. Those words heralded another change. One where she'd be alone without even the rudder of her own family. Terror held her in its grip suddenly, but she had to push through. Had to be strong. There really wasn't any other option for her. This was her lot in life.

"Indeed," she finally croaked. "Simple."

When Alric reached out and took her hand, squeezing it with a gentleness that threatened to undo the tiny modicum of control she clawed onto, she sighed. "It will be alright, Nala. I'm here. I'll always have time…"

She shook her head. "Don't promise me anything, Alric. I'm not sure I could deal with losing anything else that's been promised me." Picking up the cup, she drank slowly, until she'd drained it. Taking that time to regain her equilibrium, then she cleared her throat. "There is much still to do today."

His gaze was direct, like he was trying to divine what she thought. Maybe he desired to know what she needed. Inhale, exhale, inhale again, she thought, and instead of crumbling, Nala kept up the wall between them, determined that from this point on she would be strong, independent, and in charge of her life.

"I think we should go sort out this communicator, then I think I'd like to visit the mercantile," Nala announced.

His eyes widened then narrowed. "Today?"

She nodded. "Yes. Today. That way, if it's a shock, I will have time to come to terms with what's available before I visit with Sunny tomorrow."

"Alright," Alric answered, then he drained his cup and stood. "Let's go."

8

Alric waited until after dinner on Monday, once Sunny had left, to broach the subject of Nala undertaking the bridging course that would hopefully prepare her for the entrance exam for either nursing or medicine studies.

They'd spent long days together, he ushering her through the range of requirements for living in this new time. They included shopping for clothes—and that experience was eye opening—and working out how to use the equipment in his home, but the more time he spent with her, the more his misgivings grew.

The shop was nearly empty when they entered the mercantile, and that pleased Alric. He wasn't one for the push and hustle of sales and exotic events the stores carried on with in order to get people through the door.

Even so, he spared a thought for how Nala must be feeling, and his gaze moved in her direction. The handbag, as she'd named it, was clutched tightly in her hands, knuckles white as she gripped the straps.

"Nala?"

"I'm fine," she responded, her voice tight.

"We could do this later," he suggested, but she simply shook her head. "Fine," he muttered but took her hand in his and was grateful when she squeezed it.

"Where... Where are the ladies' clothes?" She sounded almost strangled, Alric thought.

"This way, I think." He led her to the back of the store and waited as she acclimated herself to the wide-ranging apparel on display.

"Oh, it's uh very bright," she said, looking around with wide eyes.

"Come, let's go look at the clothing toward the back." He placed his hand on her back and propelled her in that direction. "I remember Lin saying that the quieter clothes could be found there."

He watched intently as she scanned what was there. The dresses were longer and ran to darker colours.

An assistant wandered up. "Uh, can I help you?" She stared at Nala, and her clothing.

"I... uh, I need to purchase some clothing," Nala replied.

The woman scanned her clothing. "That's interesting clothing you're rocking. Have you been to a fancy dress event?"

Nala blushed a deep red, and Alric reacted by answering, "She needs some basic clothing. Dresses, skirts, pants, and tops," he growled.

The woman now shifted her focus to him, and it was difficult not to lose his temper, because he really didn't like the way she was making Nala uncomfortable.

The woman moved her gaze back to Nala. "Yes, I can see why. Dear me, you'll need shoes too," the woman added. "We should head over to the younger section, as these items are meant for the more mature ladies," she cooed.

He felt Nala stiffen beside him.

"These are fine," Alric said.

The woman started, "But..."

"Is there another server here? I think someone else would suit us better." Frustration welled inside him.

After a brief pause, the woman gave a curt nod and sauntered off.

"I'm sorry," Nala whispered. "I didn't mean to embarrass you."

"It's not you. Servers are meant to understand subtleties, and she had the sense of a brick."

Nala snorted.

"What's wrong?" He leaned down and caught sight of her slight smile.

"You were very firm with her. In a funny way," she muttered then quietened as another, older lady came over.

"How may I assist?" she queried.

This time Alric explained, and the woman nodded and smiled.

"I have some special stock. If you'll follow me this way," she murmured.

Nala had purchased several items of clothing and had been more than happy to arrange a consultation with the woman for the next day, with Sunny. Alric had reservations, but at least she was able to wear clothes that didn't quite stand out so glaringly in public. He'd also arranged a personal communication device and set up her account. The day had been successful in terms of things for Nala. So why did he feel so strange?

Nala woke up early and bathed before dressing in the new clothing she had purchased with Alric the day before. "At least I won't stick out like a sore thumb," she muttered, tugging the light blouse over her head.

The material was soft, some kind of new fabric she'd never heard of, but the woman had assured her the material wouldn't stand out. The cut was still more revealing than anything she'd worn before with a deep vee to the neckline and the short skirt, but the saleslady told her she'd just be considered conservatively dressed and a 'true professional.'

The shoes she'd chosen were a platform, according to Alric, and were appropriate for the dress, the saleslady had told her. It was the cosmetics which gave her pause, considering nice girls didn't wear them in her time.

Nala lifted her hand to inspect the applicator of lip dye and decided that was all she'd try today. Then she focussed on her hair. Rather than the customary twist she was used to, she simply brushed it down, so it lay around her shoulders.

"Well, that's as good as I can manage today."

It really was, because while she'd known and accepted the gravity, somehow looking at her new self in new clothing drove it home like a stake into her centre.

Vertigo hit, and she gripped the bench in the bathroom, breathing through the panic which seized her chest and squeezed. It took a while, breathing in and out, before the panic subsided.

Glancing up into the mirror, she saw her face. White, large open eyes. "I will overcome this," she said. "I will make a success of my new life, and I'll learn to stand on my own two feet."

9

In the three weeks since Nala had travelled with Alric, and stayed in his home, he'd simply watched her, coaxed her along the journey to finding her new life. He'd been her cheerleader, her mentor and friend. He'd grown used to her having breakfast ready when he awoke.

She and Sunny had formed a strong relationship, and it was to Sunny she deferred on things to do with clothing, hair, and the myriad social interactions, and he wasn't totally sure that was something he liked.

Nala settled in the chair opposite his as he sipped his coffee. "I thought today I should consider housing. After all," she said, then inhaled, her hand shaking, "you'll be returning to the Captivar shortly, won't you?"

Alric couldn't contain his frown. "I have another five weeks before that's due to occur. There's plenty of time."

She placed her teacup on the saucer. "I need to stand on my own two feet, Alric. All I'm waiting on are details of my medical placement, I'm now registered in the identification system, and I'm sure you've friends you haven't seen because of my presence."

He gaped at her. "Uh, no. Not really."

He really didn't have many friends, having focussed on his future during his time in the academy. Later, with the death of his father, his focus had been Linn and Sunny. If he had to count his nearest acquaintances, it would be his previous second, Jorush. But Jorush had moved to his own command, and once again, Alric was on his own. Yes, he had Shuran, but a friendship between them just wasn't a possibility.

"Alric? You do have friends, yes?"

"I have a few," he answered. "But none that would be likely to be needing or wanting to see me at this time. So, your presence isn't an issue."

Nala sighed heavily. "Fine. But I need to start my life. I need to meet people, have a home of my own and—"

"You're in that much of a rush to leave?" He spoke with irony and an arched brow, but it was tinged she thought by something else.

Fear? Loneliness?

She felt guilt at her own haste to leave. She really didn't want to, because the house was like a haven. It wasn't a case of she didn't like it here. She did. Way too much. The same as she liked Alric's attitude to life. It… It jelled with her own.

"But I don't wish to stop you living your life," she finally mumbled.

He laughed, reached over and patted her hand. Like he was older than her. It was startling to realise that he wasn't and couldn't be older than her. Because she was more than six hundred years older than him. It drew her up with a gasp.

"What?" he asked.

"I've just realised, unless I marry someone else who's a designate from an earlier year than mine, I'm always going to be older than anyone I marry." It was a strangely freeing concept. "I'm so old, I should be long dead."

He nodded. "That has occurred to me as well." He grinned. "There's many a man who likes an older woman."

"And do you like an older woman?" The words were out before she could put a cork in her mouth. She slapped a hand over her mouth.

He laughed, then that died away and a speculative gleam entered his gaze. "I... Yes, I do. I like a woman who knows what she wants. I appreciate that they know who they are. I want someone who isn't afraid to face life head-on."

Nala gulped because it was like he was describing her. She knew what she wanted. She wanted to practice medicine and have a family. She knew who she was, even if she was out of time. She was a woman with hopes and dreams. Afraid to face life head-on? She'd never really had much of a choice not to. Now that she'd embraced her reality, she was ready to get started.

"I like a man who's not intimidated by a strong woman," she told him, capturing his gaze. "I like a man who's nurturing but not smothering. One who understands women want opportunities and not to be cocooned."

Arcs of connection flowed between them, and she was sure she saw something in his gaze. Heaven knew she had butterflies in her stomach, and in that instant, if he'd kissed her, she would welcome it.

Her tongue escaped her mouth to lick at her suddenly dry lips, and she watched him follow the movement. Her breathing shallowed.

"Nala, I'm not supposed to become involved with you. I'm supposed to mentor you." But the depth of his voice was deeper and more resonant than before. Her belly quivered.

"Alric, I..." She rose slowly and he followed suit.

"If I kiss you, Nala, then we agree to pursue what this is," he warned as she stepped closer.

"Yes," she breathed.

Alric's brain bellowed 'this is wrong' but another part of him, the piece within his chest, urged him forward.

He touched her face, breathed in the scent he was coming to know as Nala. Soft, womanly. Roses.

She didn't shake or back away. Rather, she stepped boldly closer. "Alric, would you kiss me?" she breathed, and the question shot through him, zinging like a flash of electricity.

It was his time to shake, because the need inside him to be close to her was something he'd been fighting for days. Growing, deep inside, like a seed seeking sunlight.

They swayed together, and the first touch of lip-to-lip was electric. Drugging.

He sipped at her full, lower lip, not wanting to scare, and God knew, it wasn't enough, but he refused to push.

She opened her mouth and captured his bottom lip between her own.

Her taste was a fantasy, warm and rich, and he deepened their kiss, sliding his tongue within the cavern of her mouth.

He captured her in his arms, tugged her closer, diving deeper within the spell she was weaving when a sound echoed.

An insistent buzzing.

They parted, and he noted the blush on her cheeks, the heavy fall of her eyelids.

"God," he muttered, while the buzzing continued, and his brain, slowed by the sensual veil, recognised it as his communication device.

He grabbed it from the table and read the message.

"Hellfire," he muttered.

"Alric? What's wrong?" Nala's voice broke through the fury coursing in his veins.

"I… We've been called into the USF Headquarters. There's a matter of sensitivity. They don't give me any specifics. Just that we should present ourselves today."

Nala blinked. "Why?"

He sighed. "Why what?"

"Why us? Why not just you?" she answered with her own query.

"Because I chose you." When she looked baffled by his answer, he indicated she should re-take her seat. "When we bring on board a new batch of delegates, we are always looking for a leader. Someone who immediately steps up and takes control. There's always one. I think I've explained that before?"

"Yes," she replied.

"In the case of your plane, you were the one. When I boarded, you shielded the women and confronted me, even though I could see your terror. That makes you a leader. Anyway, we like to pair leaders together. It's better for training new and upcoming leaders, even if they're from the past. Those who are perceived like that will often be given a task, one that is difficult or sensitive when it involves the delegates from their group."

"Oh. There's a problem then with someone from the plane?"

He shrugged. "That I don't know. What I can say is we'd better get moving. Grab what you need in case there's an overnight stay involved."

He saw the question on her face.

"Yes, that often happens. Use the bag you'll find in the cupboard."

He waited as she left the room then cursed. The timing of this recall was awful. Not that he'd had any intention until now of acting on his interest, but to receive this summons like this?

He shook his head. "It's the way of the world, Alric."

The towering complex of the USF—United Security Forces—Headquarters for Australia was so massive Nala couldn't detect just how tall it was, and she couldn't help but stare at the facade. The building exterior was highly polished, the silver shone like a beacon. People scurried with a contained haste, while others huddled in round seating zones, talking and laughing in the courtyard, while outbuildings dwarfed by the massive tower, yet higher than she'd seen in her own time, obscured the sunlight. The heat of the noon-day sun was muted in the shaded area.

Alric ushered her inside, the revolving floor and door blocking the heat and brushing over her skin a cooling breeze.

As they stepped onto the marble floor within the building the scenery changed, and she gasped with pleasure. Scenes of Earth from varied perspectives moved slowly, as gentle music filled the air.

At the security desk, Alric waved his identification then gestured for her to do the same.

An artificial voice directed them to "elevator C" which would deliver them to the location where they'd be met. When Nala opened her mouth to enquire further, Alric shook his head, took her hand, and gently though firmly moved her to the bank of glass cabinets.

"What?" she asked, wondering why he hadn't let her speak.

"The security AI records everything said. It's better not to speak, just follow the instructions," he explained.

"What's AI?" Nala frowned.

"AI is Artificial Intelligence. We rarely use it these days though. It's an outdated technology, but until something more effective is invented the USF board of directors refuses to use humans to man security."

His answer didn't really explain what she asked, but she shrugged. Later, she could ask for more information, but right now, the cabinet opened, and he was ushering her inside.

A voice echoed, "Welcome Alric and Nala. You will be met by an escort on level seventy-one."

A sensation trickled through Nala's belly as she glanced out of the clear wall to see them rising upwards. "Is this safe?" she asked Alric, fingers scrunched together.

He gave a small laugh. "Very. This technology is also old, but well understood."

Within minutes, a ping filled the air as the cabinet slowed then stopped. The doors opened, and Alric steered her into a wide seating area.

A man strode toward them, and Nala noted with interest that Alric's grin died away to a bland and pleasant smile, which didn't show in his eyes. "Captain Eshant, this is Nala Stimson."

The man smiled, a cold façade. His face was perfect, the lines harshly symmetrical and sharp, his hair ruthlessly shaped into place, each strand straight. His silvery grey eyes chilling, and his posture unnaturally stiff. "Miss Stimson, yes, I'd heard you were designate to Alric. Come this way, would you both?"

They followed though Alric hung back slightly and that discomforted Nala.

Eshant. Of all the bad luck, that he'd be their escort, Alric snarled in his mind. He and Alric had been rivals since they'd entered the academy at the same time. Eshant embraced the 'everything by the book' attitude, unlike Alric who was more concerned with how others would be impacted and allowed that to colour his decision making.

When graduation loomed, they'd both vied for the coveted position at the flight academy, and while Eshant was a better applicant on paper, Alric had nosed forward simply because he'd embraced his empathy. Since then, whenever they'd met that rivalry had surged up.

Eshant escorted them to an office in a far corner, then followed them within. Waiting at the desk was the director of security services, Saffron McGuinness. He'd never met her before, but she was imposing, and some even went as far as to describe her as the terror of the tower.

"Captain Reys and Miss Stimson, would you please take a seat," she offered, hand gesturing to the seats, and it was clear she expected them both to oblige.

Alric waited for Nala to settle herself then took up position in the seat next to her. He was also aware that Eshant watched in silence. Alric's neck itched, but he didn't rub it. He wouldn't give Eshant the pleasure of knowing he was getting under his skin.

"We have intelligence that within the passengers aboard your plane, someone has a problem or grudge. They are attempting to remove some of their number." McGuinness rested her hands on the desk in front of them. "We don't know who it is, Miss Stimson. But the danger is growing ever more extreme. This morning one of your number was found deceased."

Nala stiffened. "Who?"

"Maxwell Grimes." Eshant's voice echoed in the silence, and Alric watched as Nala frowned.

"Maxwell Grimes. I know that name," she muttered.

"He was injured in the first week," McGuinness offered. "Along with three others from your plane." Before Nala could react or question the numbers, the woman held up a hand. "We only informed the captain after the second incidence. Over the last weeks, there have been several occasions where those from your flight have required medical attention. The one thing in common is that in each situation, it's been an accident where there were no witnesses and the injured parties have been unable... or unwilling, to tell us who was the person who perpetrated the act. Acts that have been escalating in violence."

"I don't know these people, except that we were on the same plane," Nala answered.

McGuinness nodded. "I'm aware that you were all strangers at the beginning of the flight, however, as the designate leader, we think you may be able to assist us to pinpoint our fiend."

Alric straightened in his chair. "With all due respect, director, she's not had any real contact with the other designates since her placement."

The director smiled, and it was cold. Nothing more than an uptick of the corner of her mouth. "That's why we're sending both of you on a journey."

10

Nala stared at the woman in front of her. Alric was showing due deference, yet she felt as if it were a suit he was wearing, rather than his honest reaction. And as for the other person, Eshtan? Eshant? She couldn't remember his name, and personally didn't care, but there was an obnoxious quality that she found quite unnerving.

"Designate Nala was about to begin the process of her medical bridging course—" Alric began and was cut off.

"Which can be delayed. I'm sure Eshant can make appropriate arrangements in that matter," the woman spoke drily.

Nala could feel the waves of frustration washing off Alric and wished she could support him somehow, then it occurred to her that she should support herself.

"I'm sitting right here, director, and I'm perfectly comfortable talking for myself. Until now, Captain Alric has supported and assisted me and is well aware of my concerns with integrating into society. If I were to become some kind of policeman of the other designates, as I'm assuming you suggest, then that would undermine my ability to interact with them." Nala felt somewhat pleased she'd found her voice as previously she may have simply accepted the task without remonstration.

The woman stared at her, then smiled, baring her teeth. "You don't seem to understand, Miss Stimson. This is not a request, and you don't have the luxury of refusing my demand. You are subject to all and any directive I may give, and this, my dear, is my official directive."

Alric stiffened in his seat. "She is subject only should there be aggression that may endanger—"

"You don't think this would bring the system of government into disrepute?" Eshant murmured.

"It might, but the reality is, she's not the one making the attacks. To ask her—" Alric growled.

"Enough," McGuinness called. "I can make the direction and that's what I'm doing. Captain Rey, you will escort Ms Stimson and assist her to make enquiries and find the perpetrator. Once they are identified, you will contact us." She gave a satisfied smile. "There now, my task is completed. Eshant has arranged your transport, and you will be on your way forthwith. Thank you for your time."

It was a clear dismissal, and Alric bit back an epithet because he knew there was nothing else he could do. He and Nala rose and followed Eshant out the door and into the hallway.

The man smiled as they joined him. "Here are your travel documents." He shoved a chip at them. "You're to travel to the United States, and we've allowed an allocation of up to two weeks accommodation in New York while you evaluate the situation. Daily check-ins with updates are required, and an initial booking has been made for you in the Moonbase Hotel. From there, you will be required to make any and all bookings for yourself, as appropriate." Eshant grinned. "I'm sure you'll have a successful trip." Then he walked away.

Nala turned and watched him leave as Alric seethed. "Well, that was different. I'm not sure it was quite what either of us expected, but

I guess we should find our way to the transportation…" She waved her hand. "…place."

Alric grunted. He wasn't in the mood to make happy right now. "Go this way," he said and indicated the direction of the lifts.

When she opened her mouth to speak, once they'd stepped into a cubicle, he shook his head and pointed to his ear, hoping she'd understand there were microphones within the elevator. They made the trip to the ground floor, and he pointed to the door. Nala frowned but followed his unspoken direction and headed outside.

"God damned," he grunted when they were free of the building. "Railroading us to investigate for them."

Nala frowned at him. "What do you mean?"

Seething, he considered his words before answering. "They don't want to take responsibility for investigating in case they find something that jeopardises their damned project. They have a dedicated team to deal with anomalies like this, but this situation with the designates from your plane could bring problems to the attention of the ruling government. For years they've been eliminating the recording of issues with the retrieval program. Your plane wasn't meant to be targeted. It only happened because the wormhole malfunctioned, and instead of leaving it to crash, we brought it forward. That's the unwritten and unspoken rule, but it's not a sanctioned activity. The ones we actively aim for, everyone aboard is fully investigated. Everyone. On your plane, we didn't know who we'd be getting."

She frowned. "But how would you know? I mean, we're talking hundreds of years into the past. You said yourself that there are few records."

Alric grunted. "Walk with me," he said and took her elbow. He tussled internally. Should he tell her? It was highly confidential, but she needed to know the truth, because heaven knew what the situation they were walking into would uncover. "Some time ago, our people were trialling a system, something so covert there are few of us who know. I shouldn't be telling you, but we've found a way to retrieve certain information."

She shook her head. "I don't understand?"

"We can't send people back, and heaven knows we've tried. None of our subjects survived, so we looked for ways to zero in on locations and retrieve information. Paperwork and files. But even that is dangerous. We can't afford to be seen, and we've refined our use to time our wormhole technology to arrow in on times to the minute. Each of these incursions requires weeks of preparation even though we can only open it for under a moment."

"I don't understand what you're trying to tell me," she muttered.

"Normally we begin by taking the manifest of the planes," he explained. "Then we look for details of the flight path, time of departure and so on. Our people use that to create teams who are built based on the needs of those aboard. Where there are children involved, we also look for alternatives to that flight—seeking another is always our favoured option. Your flight was an unplanned retrieval. We didn't know who was aboard. We were unprepared for the passengers, so we didn't have the information we normally would. It means we're as blind as we've been in a long time."

"So?" She sounded lost.

"We investigate the medical and mental issues of the designates. Now we have a situation we're unprepared for. Someone is actively hurting and killing passengers. Likely someone from within the passenger group."

Nala stopped and he stilled beside her, swung her to meet his gaze.

"This is dangerous, Nala. I don't know what we're going to find. Who's behind this. The director knows I entered at a leadership level, but all academy entrants undertake training in security, engineering, and science disciplines. You're not unstable or trained in areas that would assist in this situation, unless there's something I don't know? That you haven't disclosed."

She shook her head mutely.

"No. That's what I thought." He scrubbed a hand over his face. "Can you fire a gun?" Then he sighed. "Even if you can, I'm guessing it's not a laser like we have now, right? Or a stunner."

Again, she shook her head.

"Then the first step, before we begin, is we visit a shooters training centre," he growled. "I'm not taking you into a situation where you're unprepared." He took her arm. "The other thing that concerns me is that they're ducking the responsibility. By leaving it in our hands, it's not just our task, they're also making us liable."

"Pardon? I'm not sure I understand," Nala said.

He shook his head. "I need to check what's on the chip. See what written authorisation we have. But not here or now." He pulled her along the path to the transportation hub. "Once we get to New York, we can discuss it."

11

Nala settled on the bed in the hotel room, her mind whirling with the after effects of what had already been a very long day. Alric was in the room next door, but she was thankful for time to settle and think.

The trip over had been uneventful, though the strange meeting with the director and captain from the USF had seemed somewhat odd. It didn't miss her notice that Alric had been furious, though he contained his emotional turmoil. She'd become rather adept at reading him, she thought.

Her communicator blared, and she answered it with "Hello?"

Gwendolyn's face filled the screen. "Oh, Nala. Thank heavens you're safe," she cried, swiping at her eyes. "Something really bad has happened. I don't suppose…" The woman shook her head. "No, I doubt you'd be able to come."

Startled, Nala stared into the viewer screen. "I'm in New York right now. Where are you?" She wasn't going to mention what Alric had already told her, figuring that this was probably not the best way to begin an investigation. Not that she had much experience in this area. "But what's happened?"

"I don't know. I mean, we've had lots of accidents, and Roger…

He's dead, Nala! And I think..." She gulped and glanced over her shoulder, as if expecting someone to be standing there. When she looked back, her face was pallid. "I think someone is trying to hurt us."

"Send me where you are. I'll be there as soon as I can be." Nala bit her lip, holding back the information that she and Alric were there to investigate the issue.

"I thought you were safe, back in Australia, Nala. Since we've moved into our accommodations, we've been getting together..." Gwendolyn sucked in an uneven breath. "It's... I'm scared, Nala. Jane Kew, you know the blonde hostess? She was pushed off a walkway. She's in the hospital, but they don't know if she'll make it." Gwendolyn rubbed her eyes, and when she looked up, there was pure terror there.

"When did this happen and where?" Nala kept her voice even and calm though inside she was screaming.

"Last night. We met for dinner. Jane lives three blocks away, and the raised walkway takes her past the entry to her building. I saw her leave, then the group broke up. We went our separate ways. This morning the news came of her accident."

Nala's guts twisted. "You didn't see anything or anyone waiting around?"

Gwendolyn shook her head. "No, I wanted to go home. I... I'm not comfortable in this kind of society. Besides, I'm a widow. We don't carouse like that, it's not seemly or appropriate."

Nala understood. They were out of time, and the social strictures they'd been raised with were clearly so alien from the current behaviours that they felt like they didn't belong. What was the best thing to say? To ask? Confusion filled her, and her fingers tightened on the communicator.

"Oh dear, I have a meeting in ten minutes. I'll check in again later, once I hear how Jane is getting on," Gwendolyn said, and Nala could tell she was clearly trying to recentre herself. "We'll talk later." She disconnected the call, and Nala stared at the blank screen.

That was three? Four? Six? Were Jane and Roger included in the number? What if there's been others she hadn't heard of? It felt odd that someone was attacking the designates from her flight. Was there more than met the eye?

"I need to tell Alric," she muttered and turned off the screen before standing up.

A knock echoed into the room even as she reached the door. She peered through the tiny peephole just as Alric had urged her to do, and noted he was on the other side. A heavy exhalation was the only answer, and her fingers moved to the 'open door' button.

It slid open, and Alric entered with a frown. "What's wrong?" His hands reached for her, and she let him. Needed the warmth of his touch because she realised that call had chilled her to the bone.

Shivering, she shook her head, trying to conjure the words which would explain the news. "I… Gwendolyn called me." The words escaped, garbled and barely understandable.

"What?" he asked.

She cleared her throat. "Gwendolyn called me. Another designate was injured. She was pushed off the elevated walkway and is in hospital. On top of Roger…"

Alric stared at her. "Another?"

"One of the hostesses. Sarah's partner on the flight, Jane Kew. The tall, blonde woman," she explained.

He nodded. "Which hospital?"

"I… I don't know." How many hospitals were there? She hadn't asked, because in her time, there were certainly private hospitals, but they either catered to the well-to-do or in many cases specific ailments or conditions.

He must have read her confusion because he tugged her close and hugged her, and for the first time, she felt the sense of well-being she craved. "I'll find out. We'll find out who's carrying out the attacks, then we'll alert the authorities."

Alric heard his words, but it was like someone else was talking. His mind was split between the awareness of Nala in his arms and how damned right it felt. He let that feeling encompass him for another moment then set her away.

"I need to make a few enquiries. But first, tell me what you know. Did you tell her you were here?" he asked.

"I...Yes, it just slipped out." She blinked. "I didn't tell her why though," she added.

He felt pressure growing in his chest. "Okay." But he had a suspicion that whoever was taking out the others from the plane would soon learn that she was here. That would make her a target, and he wouldn't allow any harm to come to her.

"I need to get some information, but I'm worried, Nala. Whoever is after the designates will make you a target once they know you're here. All the others from your plane were placed here and now you are too."

She paled, and he swore inwardly that whoever it was had to be made accountable.

"Alric? Why would they want to hurt us? We've already lost everything that we had." Her fingers curled into tight, white-knuckled fists.

"I don't know, but we need to think. It's either another designate or one of the mentors. Nothing else really makes sense." But how could it be one of his people? They were so closely vetted for their tasks on the Captivar.

"Maybe it's just a coincidence?" But he heard the truth in her voice. She knew it wasn't someone unconnected, just like him.

He whirled away, made a call on his communicator. "I need a full list of placement mentors and designates. I need backgrounds," he demanded of Eshant.

"I thought you might. The file will be sent to your personal communicator within the hour. I've got my people pulling everything they can find on your people and on the designates," Eshant replied.

Alric frowned. "You have information on the designates?"

"Only the data we gleaned from their screening interviews at this point. My people are scanning archives, but there's not a lot to work with. A lot was damaged during the Auredian Advance."

The Auredian Advance had taken place two hundred years ago, as the struggle to create the union of planets was forming. The auredians had been determined that they wouldn't allow Earth to team up with other planets, until they'd themselves been attacked by a species intent on extermination of their kind. They'd caused immense damage, targeting the agricultural areas of the planet and areas of learning. Archives had been collateral damage, which had taken many years to overcome.

Now the auredians were among the strongest allies the earth planets had. They'd harnessed the technology of the wormhole, though they were well aware of its shortcomings.

Alric shook his head, aware that Nala was watching him. "Fine. Send through what you have now, and we'll take the rest as you find it. We know of the death, and now there's also been another attack. Jane Kew. We need to know which hospital she was taken to and if there's any vision of what took place."

Eshant sighed over the connection. "I'll get what I can, but law enforcement doesn't like to share this kind of information. I'll have to lift it covertly from their servers."

Alric understood what that meant, that law enforcement had the lead by protocol and law. "But these are designates..." he pointed out.

"And they're on the planet, Alric. You know the delineation is clear. We don't have the authority to access it officially, nor do we have the authority to interfere with their investigations. Our best bet is to shadow them. To know what they know and to keep digging."

Alric dragged his hand through his hair. "Nala could be in danger—"

"So stay beside her. But we need to know, because the danger to our society if we don't get this under control, may be far-reaching. We will not allow that. Let me be clear, if this gets out, and the populace thinks we don't have control of those who join us, we'll lose the support we rely on. Then, we believe the government will shelve the program."

Alric glanced over his shoulder at Nala, who watched with wide eyes. "Maybe we need to re-think our strategy..."

"We need this project, so we don't lose the knowledge of what came before. You know that as much as I do, Alric. Remember those extermination camps the auredians implemented? What's to stop a movement rising and determining that's how we deal with dissent? The political landscape is too fractured right now for this to do anything other than damage the agreements the parties have drawn up."

Everything Eshant stated was true. There was a movement who wanted to do away with the wormhole project. They claimed the danger to society was too great. They weren't yet strong enough, but given the opportunity...

The danger of their position couldn't be ignored. It speared him that he'd have to use Nala, and that went against everything he believed.

"Fine. Send me what you have," he said, then disconnected the call.

"Alric?" she whispered. "Is there really that much at risk?"

He couldn't miss the quiver of her bottom lip or the fear in her brown eyes.

"Yes," he said. "But they won't get to you."

She nodded and turned away, and that simple act gutted him in a way he couldn't possibly have understood before. "I'm sorry. Maybe you should have let us go?"

He had to hold onto the spike of temper that shot through him. "No, Nala."

When she turned back, tears shimmered in her eyes.

"Oh, love." He closed the distance between them and pulled her into his arms.

He wanted to say more but held onto the words because it was too much, too soon. She wasn't yet ready to hear that he wanted to explore what could grow between them. The emotions inside him had been growing day-after-day until now, but she was still lost in the haze of what-had-been. He couldn't and wouldn't push her to accept an emotion she wasn't ready for, so instead he'd wait. Be patient.

12

Alric was watching Nala; she felt the heat of his gaze as she settled at the small table with Gwendolyn. They'd chosen a small, out-of-the-way bar to meet, and Nala was pleased Alric clearly knew his way around the city so they didn't have to rely on others to help them find it.

They'd finished at the shooting range, and she'd proved a capable student. Not enough to warrant the ownership of a traditional gun, but a stunner, he told her, would be enough of a weapon for her, and he had chosen one. The waiting period would be at least a week though. He hoped they would have it before they completed their investigation, but that was out of their hands.

Now settled in the tiny bar, perched on a stool in the dimness, she and Alric waited for the cold iced teas they ordered to be delivered as she squinted at Gwendolyn who'd already been seated in the corner when they arrived.

"So, what happened to Jane?" Nala prodded the woman opposite her.

Gwendolyn sighed. "Since we arrived, we've been trying to keep in touch. You and that family are the only ones who were placed in other locations. I guess we agreed, after you left the Captivar, that it was important to stay in touch. Sarah suggested that we shouldn't totally let go of who we'd been, and we agreed. So we meet a couple of nights a week, to share what we've learned, where we're going in our plan of integration, and to remind each other of where we came from."

Nala understood those fears. She had them too, and that was why she'd set VAQU the task of finding out what she could about her family. And while a couple of grainy photos had been located, Nala hadn't gained a lot of answers as to what happened to them. A DNA sample was the next step in tracking down family members, and she'd been unsure if she was ready for that. She blinked and refocussed on the discussion.

"So, what happened? You met up and..." Nala prompted.

Gwendolyn shrugged. "We'd all found our accommodation within a couple of blocks of a restaurant near here, and Sarah said it seemed okay. Her mentor had taken her there a couple of times, and she was comfortable. We all agreed to meet there, have a meal and talk. It's pretty quiet on the nights we visit, so they agreed to give us a standing booking."

Frustration was building in Nala's veins. As a nurse gathering information, the facts in as quick a time as possible was imperative. For all that, she understood Gwendolyn needed time to work through her story, because surely there was some nugget of intelligence that they could use. She glanced in the direction of Alric who'd taken a seat beside her and let Nala lead the questioning.

"It was after nine when the group broke up. Most were walking in groups, and a few of us head in a different direction. The men offered to escort us to our doors. We feel safer like that. Anyway, Jane peeled off from our group quickly, because the overhead walkway is in a different direction. Some of the men offered to walk her, but she said she'd be fine..." Gwendolyn sniffled. "But she wasn't. Now we're scared to leave our units, because someone is waiting out there. They want to hurt us, and we've already lost two, and two more are injured, and the enforcement officers don't seem to be doing much about it."

Gwendolyn dabbed at her eyes with a handkerchief, and Nala didn't miss the shake of her fingers.

Gwendolyn speared Alric with a savage, distrustful glare. "You! You aren't doing anything about this. You brought us here against our will…"

Nala reached out and took Gwendolyn's hand. "I'm sure—"

"And you," she snarled, pointing at Nala, "you're swanning around like you're important. Why have you got your mentor at your beck and call? Hmm? Is there something more…?"

Nala pulled back, stung by the accusation. "I'm not doing anything inappropriate. Each mentor works with their designate in their own way, as you know." She tried to keep her voice even, but honestly, that Gwendolyn would even imply… Gah! She knew the words Gwendolyn was speaking was from fear, but even so, it felt like a bone-deep cut.

Alric leaned forward. "While as a designate you are provided with many things, that does not and will not excuse rudeness, Gwendolyn. Nala has been very concerned about your welfare, and it seems to me that rather than attack her, you may well consider her emotions too."

Gwendolyn slumped back into her seat with an audible huff. "And what is your concern, captain?"

Nala knew that the needling was unwarranted, so instead of allowing it to continue, she reached out and took Gwendolyn's hand. "We've made some enquiries about Jane's condition. She's been assigned a law enforcement guard and is doing as well as can be expected. They operated last night, and the pressure on her brain has eased. Her body will recover, though it will take time, so she's going to be transferred to a secure rehabilitation centre in the next few days, when she's conscious and the danger's passed."

Gwendolyn rubbed her brow. "Two dead and two injured. I don't want to be next."

Nala felt a modicum of sympathy for the woman. "I know. Alric… uh, the captain has made a request where appropriate, for designates to be re-accommodated with mentors. Where that's not possible, then a secured location might be considered."

The woman stared at Nala. "Why would you even be concerned about us? You seem to have found a sweet cushion to fall on."

Biting her lip, Nala considered the question. "There but for the grace of God," she answered.

"So, what next?" Gwendolyn asked.

Nala shrugged. "I guess we need to wait for an answer. But right now, you need to protect yourself. No more visits to the bar or restaurant. Stay home and safe." She and Alric had decided that was likely the safest option.

When Gwendolyn nodded, Nala felt a portion of the weight lifting from her shoulders.

Alric cleared his throat. "But for now, we need to leave. I have a meeting with the-powers-that-be."

"You could leave Nala here. Just for now, I mean. We could talk," Gwendolyn muttered.

Nala knew there was no meeting, and Alric was using this as a ruse, so she smiled even as she shook her head. "I need to attend it too. But I'll come by hopefully tomorrow. If you need anything, let me know."

Alric scanned the chip on his watch to pay for their order, then he and Nala rose and waited for Gwendolyn to join them. "We'll escort you home," he said.

"No," answered Gwendolyn. "I'm just over there." She waved her hand in the direction of the road. "In the tall, grey building. I can walk from here."

"We'll at least escort you to the building door then," Nala said firmly. "I'd like to know you arrived safely."

They left the small bar and crossed the busy road, and all the while Nala remained alert, looking for any kind of threat.

Once they reached the building, she took Gwendolyn's hand. "Stay inside and safe, please. There are so few of us, and we need to stay vigilant," she cautioned the other woman.

Gwendolyn stopped, sighed heavily, then turned back, shame colouring her cheeks. "Nala, what I said… It was wrong and unfair. I apologise."

Nala hugged her tight. "You're scared. So am I. Things get said in the moment."

With a nod, Gwendolyn tugged away, smiled tightly at Alric, and entered the building as they watched, then Alric placed a hand on Nala's shoulder. "You did well. We have more information—"

"Just not enough," she rebutted.

"Maybe not, but it's a start." Then he pointed in the direction of the transport hub. "We should get moving."

They moved swiftly, so that they were soon within the seething mass of people about to use the public transportation system. He guided her toward a quieter platform, and they waited for the 'swift shuttle' which in her mind looked like a pipe with small porthole windows. The side opened upwards, and he ushered her onto it, finding seats for them before once more making the payment using the chip in his wrist unit.

When she opened her mouth, he shook his head and took her hand. His was warm. Strong. The action was supportive and caring, and she swallowed the instinctive protest that rose up. Before she'd been thrust into the future, she would have remonstrated with any man who did that, but with Alric it felt strangely right.

The shuttle stopped twice before he tugged her from the seat. "This is our station," he said, and they stepped from the unit.

"Where are we going?" she asked.

"You'll see. It's a surprise," he said, and the boyish grin on his face was breathtakingly sweet.

His request of VAQU had paid off, thought Alric as he steered Nala up the stairs, her fingers twined in his. He'd taken her hand on the shuttle, knowing she still found many of the forms of transportation a trial. He'd done it to soothe her, but she'd been receptive, and for the life of him, he wasn't keen to give up the connection.

At the top of the stairs, he steered her left, toward an ancient building which had been refurbished into a combined archive and museum centre.

Once they'd entered the doors, he checked his communication

device, seeking the exact location he wished to take her. They moved through the hallway, headed for the Great Hall of Knowledge, where cubicles met them.

A man at the door, with a bored air, asked, "Do you have a booking?"

Alric nodded. "Yes. For Reyes. We're looking to examine records from—"

The man's fingers slid over the screen as Alric spoke. "Oh yes, ancient records. Post-World War II, I see. Reader cubicle fourteen is allocated. Follow me."

Nala's eyes widened as Alric tugged her along behind the man.

Alric held her close as the man opened the curtains and admitted them. "You've used cubicle readers before?"

"Yes," Alric responded and waited as the man retreated. "Come, take a seat and see what I've found."

She settled in beside him and let go of his hand so he could activate the reader. Using the holo-keyboard, Alric input the information request number and individual password.

On the screen flashed a photo of her, from the day she'd graduated from nursing school. "How...?" She turned to him, her face pale, so her brown eyes seemed huge.

"I made a request via VAQU. And as your mentor, I made a request for any information pertaining to you and your family to be eligible for printing."

She blinked. "But I thought there were strict rules governing—"

"There are," he interrupted. "But the government acknowledges the loss of history of designates, so we can request privileges." He tapped a purple icon, and a whizzing sound filled the cubicle.

On touching the small arrow on the screen, another image appeared of her family. "Your parents, sister, and brother at your memorial service. The airline did this so they could be sure, when talking with family members afterwards, that they were speaking with the appropriate people." He touched the button, and that whizzing sound came again.

He scrolled through records of her parents, sister and her family, and her brother. From time to time that whizzing sound would fill the air while Nala watched and read in stunned silence.

"My brother was a surgeon," she muttered.

"A good one, it appears. With a long history. He and his wife made tremendous strides in understanding fractures. His daughter was gifted too," Alric added.

Her sister had continued to remain in the home with their two boys, who'd both joined the Air Force, while her brother-in-law had been settled working for the bank. He'd never really risen through the ranks, and Nala guessed that suited him.

"My father lived a long life," she whispered.

"For the time." Alric reached past her and opened a small, cupboard-like receptacle and scooped up the printed images. "These are for you." He handed them to her.

Her hands shook as she took them from his grasp, and he didn't miss the shimmer of tears in her eyes. "I... Thank you, Alric. I'll treasure them." Then she glanced down at the small items in her hands.

He cupped her cheek. "I know."

She glanced up at him, and he couldn't help himself. He closed the distance between them, kissing her gently on the lips. She sighed as he brushed over the soft flesh, then Alric tugged away. "I wish I could do more."

"You already have. This means a lot to me." She smiled at him.

"I've arranged for the files to be forwarded to your communicator later today. Just in case the prints fade or you lose them at some point. They're small and..." He shrugged. What else could he say? He knew how she felt about the loss of her family. It was such a small thing he had to offer. "Anyway, we should head back to the hotel now."

They stood and he reached for the curtain, but before he could open it, she placed her hand over his. "Wait," she murmured and reached up then laid her lips against his. Heat invaded his body, and he fought the need to respond. When she pulled away, it was with flaming cheeks and bright eyes. "Thank you," she whispered.

"I didn't..." he argued.

"You did. You gave me back my family, my memories. Thank you."

Alric steered Nala into the hotel when the beeping of his communicator broke his concentration. Ushering her forward, he waited until they reached his room, the nearest to the entry, and entered it. He looked down and frowned.

<A fourth victim. Gwendolyn McCarty was attacked this afternoon. She was pushed down the stairs and her survival is unsure at this point. The injuries are extensive.>

Eshant's message had him swearing under his breath and thankful they'd detoured for the moment so they were in a private space.

"What's wrong?" Nala queried.

He refused to hide the truth from her, though it hurt him. "Your friend Gwendolyn was injured. Attacked and pushed down the stairs outside her apartment."

"But…" Shock leached the colour from Nala's skin, and she squeezed her eyes shut. When she reopened them, she appeared dazed. "We just saw her. We walked her back to the building."

Gathering her close, he held her, and noted the fine trembling of her body. "I know. But between then and now, something happened. You didn't see anyone who you knew hanging around, did you?"

She shook her head. "No, otherwise I would have said something."

He really didn't like the thoughts that were swirling around his head. The ones that had them being watched. The ones that made her a target.

13

Nala had never considered herself anything but ordinary; just a girl with a dream, who'd found a way to be more than a housewife. *I'm going to have to be more if we're going to find out who's perpetrating these vicious acts and stop them.*

Alric ushered her from his room to hers, which was next door, but it felt like walking through a dream. At least until a thought occurred.

"Can we use VAQU here? Or is it a different system? A different…" She waved her hands in the air, feeling foolish.

Alric stared at her. "What do you mean?"

"Well, we ask VAQU for assistance at home, right? But is the system here the same as the one at home?"

When Alric cocked his head, she blushed, feeling the heat scorch the skin of her face.

"It's a different system, but we can tap into our own by using our communications devices. Although, come to think of it, I don't know if yours will. They're tied to our specific homes."

"So, the one here, will it remember anything we ask? Will it be able to access the same information?" She worried her lip, waiting for Alric's answer.

"The VAQU systems here will have a lesser access, tapping into the public access knowledge banks only. Mine at home is enhanced because of my position. But what is it you want to know?"

"Well, first, I need a full list of everyone who was aboard the ship. Then I need mentor details." She turned in a slow circle, closing her eyes so she could concentrate on the facts she had, and those she needed. "I need addresses. Then we need to find out who has moved into their own locations. Then we should, I guess, talk to their mentors."

"I agree. I can make a representation for printing if you think that would assist, but Eshant has already begun the process of collating the information. We should also see if we can follow the movements of the designates. See if we can determine their whereabouts at the time of the various attacks."

She opened her eyes and looked at Alric. "We have a plan. It's not a lot, but it is a start." Agitation gnawed at her. If they failed, another would soon be injured. "The records we accessed? Can we get them for all the designates?" Her hands shook as she considered the enormity of the issues ahead.

Alric shook his head. "I pulled strings to get us what we have. This level of information is usually reserved only for scientific purposes and... But I'll make a request to see if similar information can be provided. There is some leniency for designates in the depth of information available."

Nala nodded. "So, what next?"

He sighed. "We have a couple of options. We can start by getting some food. Then eat here, or in my room, while we scan the information we have."

Biting her lip again, she considered that. "We should start on it now. At least get the information printed, so it can do ..." She shrugged, trying to find an appropriate word, but coming up with nothing. "...whatever, while we're eating." Her stomach growled. She would have ignored it, but years of medical training reinforced the knowledge that she needed to feed her brain so it would work efficiently.

"Sure," Alric answered. He opened his communicator and pressed a number of buttons in succession. "Okay, VAQU? I have queries regarding the designates of the plane C1956SAR."

"Remote authentification required," VAQU requested, the voice tinny.

"Code AR-1886-DRA-3576-Q," Alric intoned. "Request print out for all designates, mentor associations, and currently filed addresses."

"Working," answered VAQU. A long moment passed, the air thick with anticipation.

Once again, VAQU signalled, with "Acknowledged and request granted. Provide location of print output station."

Alric gave the hotel name, the room number, and her name.

"Acknowledged. Print ETA thirty-five minutes. Ensure all medium is loaded and stand by."

The connection ended, and Alric stalked to the end of the room, pressed the panel on the wall designated by a sign 'authorised personnel only' and opened it. Within was a small, silver unit and a dusty sheaf of pages.

He coughed as a cloud of dust filled the air. "They never keep these up to standard," he muttered and set about feeding the paper into a large opening in the machine. "I'll make sure the room has 'do not disturb', so no one enters or interferes with the printing process."

He left the cabinet door open and went into the bathroom, and she heard the water running and guessed Alric was washing his hands.

Alric had ushered Nala out of her room, and insisted they take a break while the printing was occurring. He wanted to make sure their night was quiet and uneventful, or at least dinner.

The restaurant was quiet, the waiters near invisible as they set about tending to the needs of their patrons. Scanning the menu, he was pleased to see a basic meal selection. The last thing he wanted was something unintelligible or avant-garde. They settled to a three-course dinner, appetisers of fried calamari, mains of beef, and a piquant dessert. The waiter bowed low, taking their drinks order then retreating.

"Tell me about your childhood," he requested.

Nala sighed. "It was during the war, in England. Not a great place to be. I remember waking up with Mother pulling us from our beds and getting us to the shelter. We didn't live in the heart of London, but the sound of the planes..." She shuddered. "The worst were the ones that went silent. You know?" Her fingers covered her mouth, and he remembered the documentaries of the ancient war which ravaged the planet. "The bombs being dropped and death and destruction. Times were hard. Food could only be purchased if you had stamps... Food stamps," she clarified.

"It was really as bad as they said?" He blinked. "I remember reading about it in my history books, but thinking they were over-stating it all."

"Oh yes, it was bad," she said, and appeared strangely upset that they seemed so remote from it, then considered it was hundreds of years in their past. "I mean, there were good things too. Like the teachers at the school I attended—they made learning interesting. We had home economics..."

"What's that?" Alric asked. The term was unfamiliar to him.

"Cooking, sewing, keeping a house. Those sorts of things. Why? What did you study?"

"We had maths, English, languages, political sciences. Then there was cultural awareness."

"Cultural awareness?" She smiled. "That sounds like it was an interesting program. Were you required to learn about Asians and native tribesmen of Africa?"

Alric sputtered, "Cultural awareness is a precursor to academy entry. It requires a dedicated study of our nearest planetary neighbours."

"Ohhh..." She blushed and the pink crested her cheekbones. "I was thinking more about here. On Earth. I didn't think... It's all a bit different. For me, I still think in small terms. I don't know if I'll ever—"

He smiled and covered the hand she'd laid on the table between them. "You've not been here all that long. Maybe you should allow yourself time for a few hiccups before you beat yourself to a pulp."

"But the others don't have that luxury."

He frowned. "You do," he insisted, because he knew what was expected of her later on. Once they'd had time to acclimate, she'd be presented to the designates court. Something she hadn't yet been informed of. Mentors usually addressed that a month or two after their designates had moved into their own homes and had completed the initial integration processes. He opened his mouth, then closed it again. Is she ready?

At least now, they didn't require the designate leaders to tell of this next hurdle. In his own mind, it had seemed an unnecessary, extra responsibility for the small group of new citizens to shoulder.

He inhaled. "There's something I haven't told you yet." Alric let the words hang in the air, and Nala's brows formed a frown.

"What?"

"Remember when you first came aboard the Captivar I said you were designated the leader?"

She nodded.

"Well, that brings with it extra responsibilities. They're not onerous, but it's why you've got extra time to acclimate. When designates are first processed, we find the leader usually is among the first to wake. Invariably, they display traits early, such as you did, shielding the women on the plane. We have a list of considerations to look for. You displayed quite a few in the first short while. It's why I chose you."

"I honestly still don't know why you chose me." She shook her head. "I'm just a woman." A gleam entered her eyes. "Was it... a sexual thing?" she whispered.

He almost laughed at her comment, but he understood she might question his reasoning. "No. Nothing like that," he answered quickly, hoping to dispel her concern. "The captain chooses the designate leader. As I said, we're trained and have a list to work through, it doesn't matter male or female. It's about understanding what makes a leader tick. And you... You were the one. But with that comes the burden of assisting with understanding the thought processes of those from your time. When one of them breaks the rules, we ask leader designates to assist, either with the judicial process, and trial, or with the investigation. I believe it's why we have been tasked with finding the attacker."

Her mouth dropped open, and clearly, she was surprised. "But... I don't know anything about any of them."

He shook his head. "You may not, but you know the time they came from. You may have some greater insight into their motivations."

She shook her head again. "No." Nala stared down at her hands. "That's not right. I can't do that. I'm not a leader, I'm just a nurse. A girl. I have no experience—"

His hand covered hers. "Nala, breathe. We can do this together. Trust me—"

She burst out of the chair, backing away. "You should have told me. What you did..."

His heart beat a rapid pulse. "Nala..."

But what could he say? Yes, he'd withheld information, and clearly, she was shocked and dismayed. Perhaps even surprised, but he didn't make the rules. This was the task he was given. Had he chosen the wrong place and time to tell her?

"Nala, I need you to understand—"

Her frustration bubbled below the surface; he could almost see it. "Understand what? You kept important information from me? You say I'm a leader, but you treat me like a weak link in a chain."

"I have clear orders. They are to prepare you for the realities of our time. You receive special privileges which allow you to acclimate fully."

"I don't want special privileges, Alric. I want to know the truth. I want to be part of this future, since I'm here without choice. I want to be controlling what happens to me."

Her raised voice caused the other diners in the restaurant to turn and look at them.

Alric rose, dumping his napkin on the plate. "Not here, Nala. Let's eat, then we can discuss it all. Upstairs." He controlled his own frustration.

She nodded stiffly, and they resumed their seats. The meal now was eaten in silence, and while frustration boiled inside him, he waited until they were done.

"Ready now?" he asked.

She nodded and stood. "I think it's time."

He took her hand. "Let's go."

Nala's eyes gleamed in the half-light, but he didn't miss the tremble of her bottom lip, nor the tension which she radiated.

Nala was furious. Steaming with frustration at the high-handed way Alric dropped the 'extra responsibilities' on her, so while fuming, she'd eaten but not tasted anything. As if it isn't enough that I was stolen from my time, my family, and the world I knew. She had to find a way to build a new life, to retrain to undertake a role she was proud of.

Everything she knew and everyone was dead. Long dead, at that. And here they were, the government or whatever, thrusting a new and definitely unwanted burden on her. Tears burned, but they weren't sadness, it wasn't even despair, but the response to the careless way they doled out responsibilities she didn't want to have to shoulder. Not now. Maybe later on, when she was ready.

She did, however, feel a chink of sympathy and embarrassment at the way she'd treated Alric. It wasn't his fault; she'd seen the restrictions he chafed against. The lack of choices. Hell, he'd even been lumped with her presence in his home. She'd bet he could have done without that too.

So, when they entered her room, she whirled around. Ready to face him, to accept the blame for her poor behaviour. But instead, she found herself plastered against his chest.

His hands caught her, so she wouldn't fall.

When their gazes met, awareness flared. Her body felt strangely warm, pliant, and soft in his arms.

"Nala…" He trembled slightly; she could feel it through the layers of clothing.

"Alric," she returned, but the sound was breathy and insubstantial, and that too was surprising.

"You feel good," he whispered, surprising her, and the trembling inside her grew.

"I…" She licked her lips and noted the darkening of his gaze, the way his eyes watched her actions. "Alric, I want…"

"What?"

They were swaying closer together and his breath fanned over her face, dark and sensual.

"I want to kiss you," he growled. "Will you let me?"

Oh God! The heat in her belly joined the tingling of other parts of her body. "Yes," she breathed, and he closed the distance between them.

The touch of his lips upon hers was a wonder. It was like melting yet becoming strong, a wind blowing wildly around her but pushing her closer as his lips roamed over hers, then deepened it. Her lips opened, his tongue sliding into her mouth and against hers in a caressing motion.

His hands moulded to her backside, holding her still and close against him, and she could feel the jut of his erection pushing against her abdomen.

The embrace came to a drugging end, and when he moved away, she felt that loss, her body cooling.

There was wonder that cascaded through her. This wasn't a first kiss, as she'd enjoyed a couple of furtive embraces before she'd begun her training as a nurse, but they'd been unlike this. She'd felt heat, passion, and hunger this time with this man. That knowledge left her stunned.

He reached up, hand cupping her cheek, thumb brushing up and down. "Where did you go just then?" he muttered, and she sighed.

"I was remembering other kisses."

He broke away, but she grabbed him.

"Not like that, Alric. I was thinking that they'd never made me feel…" She felt the flare of heat on her cheeks. "I don't…"

How could she explain the society she'd been born into, the restrictions of her chosen profession? She hunted for the right words while Alric watched her. The silence stretched out, and she needed something to fill the silence.

"I don't know what the situation is now, but when I grew up, women didn't engage in relationships with men who they weren't courting, engaged, or married to. The matron would also check regularly to see if anyone was participating in illicit relationships. They were strictly forbidden as our reputations were of the utmost importance."

He stared at her. "You are joking?"

"No. I'm really not. We had to front up regularly for checks to ensure we weren't doing anything inappropriate. And by inappropriate, I mean, being seen out with a man or consorting with people of ill repute. Most of us would go out in groups, but we lived at the hospital, so we were watched carefully."

"I can't… You were adults," he sputtered.

"Times were different, Alric. This? I'd be removed from my post if this had occurred. Being in a hotel room with a man who wasn't my brother or father would have caused all kinds of issues."

He smiled, his lips lifting at the corner slowly, as his eyes glinted. "Then you should enjoy this," he said and swooped in again, capturing her mouth.

Her brain switched off as she enjoyed the pleasure of the touch, the heady taste of him. The kiss deepened as fire flashed through her veins, urging her to grab onto him, fingers curling into his broad shoulders.

When Alric groaned and lifted his head, she had the distinct sensation of being drugged, her eyelids felt weighted, and her body ached for more. "Oh, Nala, what you do to me," he muttered.

"I don't know what I might be doing to you, but I…" she gulped, trying to find the words to explain the emptiness inside her, the hunger building.

He rested his forehead against hers. "You're not ready, and we have a mess on our hands we need to settle first," he said, but she didn't miss the frustration threading through his voice.

"Perhaps we should call it a night?"

"No, Nala. We need that list, and to get some ideas." Alric tugged away and stalked to the cabinet, withdrawing the paper list.

She reached into her handbag and tugged out the pencil stub as he settled at the small table. "Come join me and let's begin."

They started by crossing off those either deceased or injured. "Clearly, they aren't our perpetrator," Alric growled, but that left a long line of possible suspects, not including the children. "They were sent to Washington, along with their parents, and I believe are involved in an intensive family training program."

"So, Susan and Fred can't be involved?" Nala queried.

"I'm not sure, but I'll contact the unit and make some enquiries. However, I'd say for now, we can discount them."

Nala placed an asterisk next to the parents' names and drew a line through the children's. It wasn't a lot, but better than nothing.

"We don't have a lot of information," Nala said, scratching her neck.

"No. Look, we've made a start, let's leave it at that tonight, and tomorrow I'll bring up a holo-map, and we can work out who's living where. Maybe there's some kind of clear hint in their locations." Alric didn't sound overly hopeful though.

"We can do that. Uh, Alric?"

His gaze zeroed in on her.

"Maybe we could have breakfast here tomorrow, while we work?" She spoke quickly and had to contain a wince when the words ended in a squeak.

He nodded. "I'd like that, Nala."

Four words were all it took for her body to flame again. It was heady to know there was desire on both sides. The only question was 'what next?'

When Alric stood, she made to rise, but he shook his head. "Stay there, and I'll see myself out."

Nala bit her lip and nodded.

"I'll be back in the morning. Is eight too early?"

Now, Nala smiled. "It feels positively slothful. I used to rise between five and six to prepare for work."

"I can come earlier, if that suits?"

Did it? He'd be here sooner, so the time apart would be less... She blinked, aware that her thoughts were straying in a direction she'd never allowed them to. "Maybe seven, if that is fine with you?"

He gave a curt nod, but it was the heat still burning in his gaze that warned her he was biding his time. Waiting until she was ready for the next step.

That sense of power was heady. "Good night, Alric."

"Good night, Nala," he replied and headed for the door. He had it open and had stepped out, before turning back. "Maybe..."

"Maybe what?"

"Dream of me, Nala." Then he smiled and shut the door.

"Oh Lord, I'm in big trouble," she whispered.

14

Alric rose early and settled into stretching, just as he did every morning, but the entire time he was aware of the passing of minutes. Once finished, he showered and dressed, every few minutes checking the time, and by six forty-five he was climbing the walls.

"This is ridiculous," he muttered out loud. Anyone would think him a schoolboy waiting to meet with his crush. The thing was, the emotions which swirled inside him were deep, like the vast ocean, and he wasn't sure where, or if indeed, they did end.

All he knew, with certainty, was that unlike other women, Nala was one he just couldn't spend enough time with. She was bright and interesting. The stories she told him of her life previously unwrapping a period they had little written history of.

At six-fifty, he stalked to the door. "Damn this waiting."

He marched down the hall to her room. Knocking briskly, he waited for the 'come in,' and when the light on the privacy panel switched to green, he pushed the door open.

Nala waited for him, wearing a conservative purple pantsuit. The colour highlighted the creamy tones of her skin. Her hair was fastened back in a style that framed her face, gentle and womanly.

"Good morning, Alric," she said with a husky tone.

The sound shattered the fragile attempt to control his hunger, and he stalked toward her. "Tell me you don't want this," he muttered, giving her a moment to respond.

She did, reaching up to grasp his shoulders and laying her lips against his.

Lust speared him, his body already tight, and his grasp on his appetite for her was tenuous.

Kissing her, feeling the soft pads of her lips beneath his was a pleasure he doubted he'd ever tire of, and the way her body moulded against his increased his heartrate to a frantic gallop.

Her lips opened for him, and his tongue surged into the warm, honeyed cavern of her mouth, and Alric stroked her tongue with his. There was no denying that he wanted her frantically, but there was an awareness that she wasn't ready, and he would be stupid to push her to an intimacy before she agreed to more. Because in his mind, there was so much more at stake than a casual sexual encounter between consenting adults.

He pulled away, though his body screamed at him to continue the embrace. "Damn," he muttered.

"Something like that," she whispered, and he groaned a laugh. "That was a hell of a way to say good morning," Nala added.

He took her hand and tugged her to the table. "Sit down before I pounce," he muttered and dragged his fingers through his hair as he fought to control himself.

She did, though not without a coquettish smile. "I slept well, how about you?"

"I didn't. I tossed and turned most of the night, thinking about that kiss. Does that surprise you?"

She blushed and dipped her gaze.

"Nala?"

"I... I dreamed of you," she answered, and he leaned in, intrigued.

"What did you dream?"

The rosy hue on her face got redder. "Us. Kissing. You, touching me..." Her words trailed away.

His groin ached. "How?" His tone was guttural as he demanded more information.

"Your hands on my skin. My… my breasts," she whispered.

"Does it make you hot?" He leaned across the table and grabbed her hands when she raised them as if to cover her face.

"Yes. I… I wanted more. I wanted you to make love to me."

He had to close his eyes, count to ten. When he opened them, she was staring at him.

"Does that… Does that disgust you?"

He shook his head. "I'm so hard right now, I would burst if you touched me," he answered honestly.

"Oh…" She glanced down, but thankfully, the table obscured the truth of just how erect and ready he was. "Oh, well, I guess…" She licked her lips, and he couldn't contain the groan as it erupted from him.

"Sweetheart, you're killing me," he growled.

"I've never… No man has ever said these things to me. I'm at sea. I don't know how to respond, Alric."

Once more, he closed his eyes and counted. "You're not doing anything wrong, and as for a response, there's more than one, but they probably all end up at the same point. Me with you, naked and in that bed."

It was an effort to force the words out, but he opened his eyes and waited for her reaction. Noted the echo of desire, the way her mouth opened a little, her lips pouty. He could crawl across the table right now and she'd likely not fight him, but that wasn't what he wanted. If Nala and he were to have sex, he wanted her willing, hungry, and fully engaged. In more ways than one, he conceded.

Regrets weren't high on his list of favoured emotions.

"We should… We should order breakfast," Nala mumbled.

"Yes, we should." He pressed the button on the table and the holographic menu appeared. "What are you hungry for?"

She giggled, and for a moment, he stared at her, then joined in. When the laughter died away, some of the tension in the air had evaporated. They made their order, then he picked up the papers he'd left on the table.

"We should consider those on the plane while we wait," he said. "I'd like your impression of them."

Nala rubbed her brow. "I'm not sure how useful that would be. I mean, I've only known them a short time."

He shook his head. "You have a knack for people, Nala. Besides, while I have access to their records from the processing, it's all cut-and-dried. People can and have 'beat' these tests before. If you consider the questions, they're easy to address and give a false reading."

He began listing the names and waited for her response. "Pithy and curt," she named one, another was "obsequious." Alric raised his brow at that but continued. "Shy and retiring," she described the older lady on the manifest. "Gwendolyn is a widow, she keeps a shell around her, but inside she's just terribly lonely, and Sarah is odd. She's hard and brittle, but also wants to be at the centre of attention. She's probably the hardest to read," Nala added.

He frowned and made a notation beside the women. They'd only got halfway through the list when the room VAQU informed them that breakfast was waiting.

Nala made to rise. "No, I'll get it," he said and ambled for the door.

Outside, a man waited with a trolley and a range of domed dishes. "I'll set them out," the man said quietly, and Alric stepped back, waiting by the door until the server had completed his task and left the room.

"So next..."

Alric shook his head. "Put it away while we eat, then we can continue."

Nala blinked and slid the papers into her handbag along with the pencil. "Tell me, do you love what you do?"

"Pardon?" He stopped in the process of removing one of the domes.

"Do you love your job? I know you're the captain of the Captivar, but what is it about your job that makes you feel fulfilled?"

"Since I was a boy, the planets have been my friends. My father was a captain when I was born, and later, he rose to the rank of admiral. My family had been involved with the interplanetary negotiations, and I guess I knew when I was young it was where my future lay."

"Hmm. So, is that what you're doing now? I mean, it seems you don't get out there..." She waved her arm at the roof. "Don't you wish you could go further?"

The question surprised him, and he had to think hard about his answer. "I'd love to travel further, but when the position of captain came about, there weren't a lot of opportunities. Most of the fleet were in mothballs and it's only in the past three years that there's been a push to build more ships. But I'm committed to the Captivar for another year or eighteen months. The placement rotation is five years."

"Oh," she muttered. "Is that for all crew or just captains?"

He laughed. "Captains. Crew are rotated depending on need, personal circumstances, and skills. Why?"

She bit her lip. "Well, once I begin training, I noticed that I need a placement. I'm trying to work out my options."

He stilled, wondering what she was thinking.

"I'd thought about applying to be placed aboard a fleet ship, but..." She coughed, covered her mouth, and looked away.

"Nala, what were you thinking?"

"I wondered if I should ask... If it would be appropriate to consider the Captivar."

The words were impactful. "To stay with...?"

"I don't want to be pushy, but things are... Oh, dear Lord, this is difficult," she muttered.

"You want to be with me?" he asked, hopeful that was what she was thinking.

"I, uh, yes. But if you're not interested, then tell me," she hurried to answer.

He smiled. "What do you want?"

Nala gulped. "I don't know," she whispered, and she blushed a deep red. "I'm being too forward," she muttered.

He placed the dome on the table and reached for her hand. "Not at all. Yes, if you want that, I'd be very pleased. But you don't have to decide immediately. Now eat, and we can discuss this later."

It wasn't that he didn't want to discuss it, he was elated that she was considering being close to him, but right now, everything between them was uncertain. There was training to undertake, a killer to find, and her acclimation into a society she was unfamiliar with to complete.

Besides, while he wanted her, he didn't want her decision clouded by lust. Nala deserved better than that.

But even so, the thought continued to swirl in his head while they ate in near silence.

Nala was pleased to end breakfast, given the conversation. It wasn't that she didn't want to talk about it—hell, she was the one who'd raised the topic—but how far was it seemly to push?

After breakfast, she absented herself to use the facilities and took a moment to look in the mirror. "Mother would be horrified," she told herself.

But the reality was her mother wasn't there, and the world had changed. Besides, it wasn't like she was jumping naked in his bed. Yet, her brain added.

Inhaling deeply, Nala rinsed her face, brushed her hair, then reached for a dentatab and swallowed it. "So much quicker than needing to brush," she muttered as she left the bathroom.

"Everything fine?" Alric queried as she left the small room.

"The whole dentatab thing is great. Just swallow, and no brushing. Whoever invented those is a time-saviour."

Alric laughed. "Dentatabs have been around a long time. I don't know who invented them, but I would imagine that brushing would take time."

So many changes, and she needed to shed the shackles of a long-forgotten time, she guessed.

"You know, while there's likely to be a wealth of new experiences for you, you don't need to absorb them all. There's things that you do, like the way you cover your mouth in the morning, that are sweet and part of who you are. Don't change you, just to keep up," Alric said.

She stared at him, because it was like he could read what she was thinking. Maybe he can? Nala discounted that, because she'd never seen any indication that was a real thing.

"Nala?" He watched her, a frown on his face.

"I'm just wool gathering, sorry."

He looked confused. "Wool gathering?"

She giggled at the confusion on his face and the way his brows squashed together. "It means I'm off with the fairies."

He continued that look. "Fairies?"

Inhaling deeply, she tried to think of how to explain it. "I was thinking about something else. A bit of whimsy, if you will."

"Oh. Now I understand. Wool gathering, huh? Off with the fairies. I'll have to bank those phrases for later use."

She wasn't sure how she felt about that. No doubt he found them quaint, but they were a part of who she was and the time she was from. If I dwell on that, and let that colour all our discussions, it will drive me mad.

"Nala?" he asked, as if he could tell she was discomforted by his comments.

"It's fine." She turned away. "We should look at the information we didn't consider last night."

"Wait, Nala. Did I say something?"

Feeling like she was being unfair, she turned back. "I'm struggling a little with your comment about the way I speak. I know it's different, and I recognise that it's my issue."

"I'm sorry, I didn't mean to upset you, Nala. I didn't think…" He shrugged.

She sighed, aware that she probably sounded silly and pedantic. "No, I need to stop being so on edge about these sorts of things."

He crowded in, enveloped her in his arms, and she settled against his chest. "I'm sorry. I didn't realise just how hard it was for people to make the transition until I met you. I... Can I just say, though, that you have made me understand just how difficult it is."

The beat of his heart settled the frustration which had crashed down on her, and she shuddered, feeling the sense of contentment she'd been missing. She soaked it up for long moments, but finally, she realised time was sliding away. "We should get into the list," she muttered, and he released her.

"Let me clear the table, and you get the papers," Alric said.

They cleared everything quickly, and finally, they settled back at the table.

She spread the papers between them, and she scanned the information included in the columns. "I have the names, their mentors, and addresses. I think you said you could bring up a map?"

He smiled and laid his communicator onto the table. A quick touch of the screen and a map appeared in the air between them.

"I'm never going to think this is an everyday thing." She smiled.

"The hologram?"

She nodded. "They didn't have those back in my time. And I think I need to come up with a way to stop saying 'in my time.'" I'm not going to be going back. I need to stop calling it 'my time.'

"It's something we usually learn in the classroom, but if that's also new to you..." He shrugged. "I can teach you how to use the program if you like."

"I guess that would be useful," she conceded. "But maybe later. Let's get the placements on the map and see what we can discern."

She listed the addresses, and they colour-coded them in red for females and blue for males. The accommodation units, she noted were in clusters. Three and four per building, and she frowned. "They're grouped."

"You think that's odd?"

"Not really, I suppose," Nala answered. But she wondered if units were kept empty specifically for these kinds of situations. "I guess, looking at the way they're clumped together, it makes me wonder how you have that many in the same place. It's either females or males for the most part, except here." She pointed to one area particularly.

"The government mandates that any new building has a percentage of open units to ensure housing for those in immediate need."

"That's very forward-thinking, isn't it?" Nala asked.

Alric frowned. "I don't know why you'd say that as it's a historic ruling for building applications." He ran his hands through his hair. "So, how do you want to arrange the mentor interviews?"

Biting her lip, Nala squinted at the map then glanced at the list. "The mentors are all still available to the designates, yes?" She looked to Alric.

"Not necessarily. Once designates are rehoused, quite often they return to work, though they are not sent off planet, if that's their usual place of employment."

"Okay, so there's no reason we shouldn't be able to request a meeting. I think we should begin with those who mentored designates that were hurt or deceased," she said with a wince.

"Are you alright?" Alric queried, clearly realising she was upset by the situation.

Rubbing her hand over her eyes, Nala sighed. "Yes and no. I've seen the results previously of the evils men can visit on their peers. I'm no stranger to that. However, previously, I haven't personally known those before the incidents that land them in the hospital." It was difficult to explain the depths of her emotions.

15

Alric ushered Nala toward the front of the building later in the day. "I've arranged for us to meet with the mentors in a cafeteria. I thought it would be less intimidating."

She nodded, and he noted her stiff posture.

In truth, he was aware of the toll this whole situation was taking on her. First being thrust through a wormhole and now needing to find the person or persons who was attacking and ultimately killing, but he couldn't make it better.

"Come this way," he said and pointed to the arrow that indicated where the cafeteria was.

They entered the bright and airy café. She stopped, stared. "I've never been in a place like this before," she said, and he realised it was yet another first for her.

"These areas have resumed their popularity in the last century. They were common meeting areas in the late twenty-first and into the twenty-second century."

"I see," she muttered. "Well, we should meet the people we came to see."

His hand touched her stiff back and pointed her toward the back of the room, where a small group waited. He knew one of the mentors, as he worked in the engineering department of the Captivar.

The man stood and extended his hand. "Captain, I was surprised to hear from you."

"Thanks, Verno, I was sorry to hear of your designates' death," Alric said as he shook the man's hand.

"It's not the outcome anyone would have hoped for. But the law enforcement officers indicated they felt it was simply an accident."

Alric didn't say anything to correct the man's belief. That would come once they'd worked out the who and what of the situation.

Alric introduced himself and Nala to the rest of those gathered. "Thank you for joining me," he said. "I was asked to discuss with you all about how the situation with your designates was going. Verno, I know your situation is a little different, but we didn't want to ignore you under the circumstances."

Verno inclined his head, while Nala fidgeted beside Alric. He knew she was itching to ask questions, but he laid his hand covertly on her lap, reminding her that patience was important.

"Why were we called together, captain?" another mentor queried as Alric ordered drinks, and he noted the others were already sipping at juices or other non-alcoholic beverages.

"We needed to check how your designates are managing," he answered, not that this was the whole truth.

The woman opposite him frowned. "I've had three previous designates, and this has never occurred," she muttered.

Alric understood her confusion, but both he and Nala had agreed he needed to keep the truth of the situation under wraps. He cleared his throat and said, "This is the first time I've been the apex mentor. I feel that it is in everyone's best interests to ensure that the designates are acclimating well."

"Verno's isn't, so why is he here?" the woman growled.

"Because, although his designate has died, I need to ensure the process is optimal for us and them."

"Is that why you brought your designate then, captain?" the second man queried.

"No. I'm acclimating Nala as she's a leader designate," Alric answered.

"Ah," the woman said. "So, she's not here because of something more…"

The insinuation burned him, but he had the distinct impression the barb hit deep for Nala, in the way her muscles tensed.

"That's unnecessary and inappropriate," he growled. "We should be concentrating on the matter at hand, which is the acclimation of your individual designates. Elana, how is Jennifer settling?"

He saw the woman wanted to say more, but subsided.

Elana looked from the woman to him. "Fine. She's got an educational plan in place and has moved to her unit nearby. She's integrating slowly, and that's impacted by the group's insistence on their regular 'stay in touch' meet-ups."

Alric didn't miss the sourness in her tone. It gave him pause. He'd do more about looking up Jennifer once the meeting was over. He asked another man, who gave a quick but hopeful rundown. He too made comment on the meet-ups, and stated it was one of the women who initiated the meetings.

Slowly, one by one, Alric enquired of them all who were present, as some had been unavailable, making notations. He made a mental note to check in the designates once the situation was sorted. He had questions about making sure the system worked for the designates too. Perhaps there were other ways to choose mentors for designates that might improve their outcomes? What if the best mentors weren't on the craft at the time?

Alric lifted his drink to his lips, as Nala did the same. He drained his cup and set it down. "Alright then, thank you for taking the time to talk with me. I'm hoping to get around to all the mentors in the next day or so, but I'd prefer if you kept the content of these meetings to yourselves. It occurs to me some of the designates may feel uncomfortable if they're aware we're discussing their integration into our society. I'd like to keep the impact as low as possible."

Murmurs swept around the table, though he didn't miss the gleam in Elana's eye.

"Elana? I really mean what I say about the confidentiality. If I get so much as a whiff you've said anything outside the group, I will take it up with the central agency."

Her lips thinned as did her brows, but she nodded her agreement. It wasn't a perfect outcome, but he could live with it. She'd not asked her questions, and he knew she too felt that the questions for the designates was as important, if not more so, than the mentors.

Looking at Nala, they rose together and left the building in silence.

Later in the day, they met with the next group of mentors, and Nala wondered if there was anything useful to be gleaned from the meetings. At the end of the day, they collapsed in the chairs in her room.

"That was a waste of time," she groused.

Alric shook his head. "Not at all. We know one of the women was the instigator of the meetings by the group. We know that there is no single point of interest that indicates the reason behind the incidents, or at least from the understanding of the mentors."

"Great, so we know what we don't know." She leaned back in the seat.

"What it tells us is these aren't avenues of interest to us. What we really need to find out now is why someone would want to get rid of others from the plane? What is the benefit for them? And while we haven't yet removed many from the list of suspects, we have more information. Our next step after we finish with the mentors is to work out the whereabouts of our suspects."

Nala rolled her eyes. "How do you plan to do that?" She scrubbed her hands over her eyes.

"We make a request through Eshant for the details of their communicator numbers, then we track their movements for the last forty-eight hours."

"How would you do that?" She blinked.

"We'll request the data through the government officials. From our perspective, it's simple."

She wondered just how simple that could be. She really didn't understand a lot of the processes involved, nor did she understand the basics of the technology.

"I know it's a lot for you to take in, but it is really that simple. The use of communications systems leaves a mark on the digital records, like finding a fingerprint. Systems techs can follow the location of the device by a process of basic triangulation, worked out by noting which bases delivered data packages to the devices," Alric explained, drawing in the air.

"I don't understand half of what you just said, but I believe you. You seem to know how these processes work." Nala felt as if she were totally incapable in a world that relied on these foreign communications concepts.

"You'll get there, Nala. It'll take time, but you will grasp it. Amelia Earhart is now a systems analyst, so there you go."

He smiled, and she was sure he thought that made her feel better, but it only reminded her that somehow, she couldn't understand the complexities of the communications systems.

"So, what now?" she asked.

Alric looked at his chrono—it was more than a simple watch, she'd learned since her arrival—and frowned. "It's too late for us to track down any other mentors today or to catch Eshant, so I guess, we make a plan for tomorrow." He settled beside her. "I know it all seems overwhelming." His arm wound around her shoulders and pulled her in tight. "Believe it or not, we've achieved quite a bit. Most investigations take days when there is no clarity as to who the perpetrator is. This person has already assessed where video feeds are streamed from and is either hiding from them or obscuring themselves somehow. And given how many possible suspects we have..."

The words hung in the air. "But what if someone else is hurt, Alric?" She shook her head. "I can't help but feel responsible."

He sighed and the sound filled the room. "You're responsible how, Nala? Did you attack them?"

She stared at him for a long second. "No!"

"Then you aren't. I'd rather be further along too, but we must be realistic. Time is on their side now, but we'll find them. We'll stop them. It just takes..." Alric shrugged.

Neither of them finished the sentence, but the word hung there. 'Time.' The one thing someone didn't have.

She turned and curled up in his embrace. "I wish..."

"You wish what?"

Squeezing her eyes shut, she made a noise between a laugh and a hiccup.

"Nala?"

She raised her head, stared into his eyes. "I wish I'd been born in this time, so I wouldn't have to feel like I'm odd. I wish I could..." Nala moved, covering the distance between them and kissing him. Trying to infuse into the embrace the depths of both her confusion and wants.

He remained still, and she pulled away. "I shouldn't have done that," she muttered.

His hands gripped her shoulders so she couldn't retreat further. "Tell me what you wish for, Nala."

The heat of her blush scorched the skin of her cheeks, and she tried to retreat, but he held her in place.

"What do you want, Nala? Tell me."

There was a strangely hypnotic tone in his voice, and she whispered, "I wish I could be with you." The words escaped almost inaudibly, as if they'd been prised free through some tiny crack in her psyche.

"Why can't you be?"

Him being so forward shocked her. Now she looked for a hint that he was joking, playing with her, but nothing was there, only openness and honesty.

Her heartrate increased, blood thrumming through her veins. "I..."

"Nala, you can be or do what you want. If that's with me, then there is no impediment, except the ones in your mind. I don't believe in indiscriminate sex. For me, it's an aspect of a relationship, and those I take seriously."

Swallowing, she tried to think sensibly, to consider his words, but until recently she'd lived in 1956 and those social mores chained her to a standard of behaviour. "I wish… I know you…" Rolling her eyes, she tried to come up with the words to explain and failed.

"I know, Nala. Besides, you aren't ready yet." He smiled and his lopsided grin made her feel even more conflicted.

"You don't understand. The confines and restrictions on women of our time meant that we… I've never been with a man," she blurted out then ducked her head, because she'd admitted something that was kept between a husband and a wife. That, they certainly weren't.

"Then if or when it happens, I will treasure your gift, Nala. By our standards, I'm old-fashioned. When and if we engage in a physical relationship, it will be with the view that we are building a shared future."

She had the distinct impression he wanted to say more, but long seconds of silence passed before he shook his head.

"Alric?"

"Neither of us is ready, Nala. You need to get to know me, and I have a duty to assist you. We also have this investigation, but I do want to be with you—don't be under any illusions about that."

Nala blinked. *How do I respond to that?*

With slow movements, he tugged away and rose, and for the first time, she noted a stiffness in his gait. Her gaze was automatically drawn to his groin, and she saw the bulge that clearly declared his sexual interest. "Oh…" she whispered, and her gaze rose to his face.

He smiled, and she could tell that he knew what she'd seen. "One day soon, Nala. Now, we should go find something to eat."

16

Alric wasn't sure how best to proceed with Nala. He understood the conflicting emotions she was experiencing, and he was happy to wait, but she'd advance and retreat, in a dance of awareness.

His body still ached. The desire he struggled to repress was becoming more urgent as each day with her passed, but he was determined to do the right thing, to follow his conscience.

They'd kept their conversation over dinner light, and he'd suggested they both should have an early night. Her ready agreement reinforced that his was the right plan for now.

Tonight, he would research what little was known of her time. On a whim, he sent a message to his sister Sunny.

<What information do you have on the social culture of the 1950s?>

Once that was sent, he attended to his ablutions, aware that in the room next door, Nala was likely doing the same. "Torturing yourself isn't going to help," he muttered, resting his forehead against the cold, ceramic wall.

Once he'd dressed, he settled on the bed and noted that Sunny had responded.

<There isn't a lot. We have some basic understandings around morality, dress, and social restrictions that usually applied to females. I'm guessing you want specifics, so try these museum links.>

He saw there were three, and he slowly clicked on the first one, wondering if Nala would think this was an invasion of her privacy.

The screen opened with a black backdrop, and a woman walked across it. She smiled, waved, and clicked her fingers. The front of the museum filled the screen, and she made her way through the front doors and into an alien section with a large, wooden unit, boxy chairs covered in fabric, and a man, woman, teenaged boy, and younger girl.

"Welcome to the Museum of Ancient Democracy. I'm going to walk you through a special exhibit today, focusing on the post-World War II era, known as the 1950s. This was a time of repositioning.

"The clothing the family wore was alien, heavy with brown and khaki tones. The men in pants and checked shirts, while the females wore voluminous skirts and tailored tops.

"The furniture was predominantly wood, and the soft furnishings tones of turquoise and muddy yellow, and figured heavy decoration on the walls of similar tones, usually wallpaper.

"During the war, only men were fighting, but that left a gaping hole in industry, so women entered the workforce, undertaking what had traditionally been classified as male tasks. By the 1950s though, women had returned to the home. Their tasks were as homemakers. The highest most women could aspire to was the role of mother and wife, and women took great pains to ensure the husband and children's needs were foremost in their mind."

The man and children disappeared from the screen.

"Men would head to work, the children to school, and the women would remain at home, cleaning, shopping, and for those who were inclined, the task of making their own clothes were pivotal to their sense of self."

The woman was now pictured busy in the kitchen, preparing vegetables, while overdressed with makeup and her hair carefully styled, a string of pearls at her neck and smaller ones in her ears.

"Women were encouraged to ensure that all aspects of their grooming were considered, even while attending to the housework."

Alric paused the video and sent Sunny another message.

> How accurate is this data?

Her response came quickly.

> We believe it's fairly accurate. Discussions with those who we retrieved from the 1950s and the documents and videos which have survived reinforce these beliefs.

He shook his head and set the transmission to play.

"Footage was recently retrieved from an old system of communication which encouraged women to always prepare appropriately for sewing, for example. In the video, we see a woman with immaculate hair and makeup being encouraged to prepare for the experience."

A grainy black-and-white video played in the corner of the screen.

"Of course, some women remained in the workforce. This was a minority, and they usually undertook tasks such as nurse, server, housemaid, or teacher, but they were considered inferior to the males engaged in similar tasks. Women in the workforce, particularly in offices, were required to wear heavy uniforms, often of wool, and were subjected to stringent morality checks. They were required to remain unmarried and many of these women were denied a family as it was believed they chose a 'profession' or 'career' over the natural role as a nurturer."

Alric turned the video off, having seen enough.
"No wonder she's so unsure."
He checked the next link, and it was a written description of family life and social restrictions women chafed under. He noted the fact that

women who intended to marry 'courted,' and that was usually a precursor to marriage. Once a woman was engaged, she was required to plan the wedding in short order, as her chastity—the act of refraining from sexual activity—was considered vital.

The picture it evoked was a society that didn't allow women the ability to grow and think for themselves. It was restrictive and shallow. He now began to understand why Nala reacted as she did.

In effect, the placing of her with a male mentor put him in the role of her father. That wasn't something he was comfortable with at all. "No, that's not right," he muttered to himself. "I'm not her father, and the way I feel is distinctly un-father-like." All he had to do was consider how hard he got every time they kissed.

He crawled into the bed, aware he'd need to consider what they did next, how to approach the investigation, and at some point, he'd need to clarify what they both wanted to learn about their emotional connection.

Nala waited impatiently while the mentors before her fiddled with their communications devices. Alric had absented himself to take a message from Eshant.

"Why do we have to be here?" muttered one of the women.

"The captain will be back in a moment," Nala replied, hoping that was in fact the truth.

Alric strode into the restaurant they'd met at. "Apologies, but that was an official communication," he said. He looked strained. The corners of his mouth tight and white.

Her immediate impulse was to go to him, put her arms around him, but she restrained it as he took a seat beside her.

"We're here today to discuss the designates you've been allocated," he said.

They'd discussed the situation and felt that perhaps more clarity around the information they sought would help them settle on possible perpetrators.

All eyes were now on Alric, and the silence stretched.

He'd used this routine before, maybe not with such a clear-cut description. Previously, he'd taken a softly-softly approach, so she guessed whatever he'd been told during the discussion had been bad.

He started asking questions, waiting for answers around their impressions of designates, and she watched him in action, and checked the mentors' facial expressions to see if she could discern their feelings. By the end of the meeting, she was just as frustrated as she'd been at the start.

"Nothing," she muttered as they once again entered the hotel. "They had no information for us. They all looked surprised when you explained the severity of the attacks, but no one looked guilty or…" She shrugged.

"We had to cross everyone off that was on the mentor list, and now we've done that. You take the lead with the designates."

"Me?" Her voice rose.

He nodded. "Yes, you. They know you, Nala. You're one of them. A designate." Alric frowned. "We just need to improvise an opportunity to get you—"

Her communicator cut through the discussion. "It's Sarah," she muttered.

"Answer it," Alric instructed, and she did.

"Oh, Nala! Gwendolyn's been hurt, and I… I wish you were here. You'd fix it, like you did everything else."

"I didn't fix anything," she answered, glancing at Alric who was watching intently.

"Yes, you did. You became the leader of all of us, and we need you now. Can you come?"

Nala winced, but Alric nodded and mouthed 'yes,' so she responded, "Of course I can. When?"

"Can you get here tonight? We're all meeting at the restaurant we've started frequenting. There's a hotel nearby. It's not big, but I'm sure you could gain accommodation. Please?"

Nala sighed. "Sure. Send me the details, and I'll get there as quickly as possible." A lump grew in her stomach from the lie. Clearly

Sarah was distraught and needed the support, and she wanted to give it, but a chill lodged in her spine.

After she disconnected the call, she stared at Alric. "Well?"

"We move hotels. You go to the restaurant, and I'll shadow you. You act as if you're on your own, but you won't be. I'll be there the whole time, and I'll call in backup from Eshant. You'll be safe, Nala, but we need this opportunity."

She chewed her lips. The thought of being bait for whoever was the person injuring them, especially when she was aware it was someone from within the group, made her feel positively nauseous.

"Alright then. We move today."

Alric growled as he paced the new hotel room. While the building was quaint, the room was bijoux at best, and as there was only one available, he and Nala were now sharing.

She'd disappeared into the bathroom, ostensibly to change for the meeting tonight, and he frowned at the communique from Eshant. There would be no backup at this point, since the plan was ad hoc according to the man. There's too many variabilities.

That response was a cop-out. That's why Alric had requested assistance, but there wasn't going to be any. So instead, he'd have to shadow Nala closely from the hotel to the restaurant and back again.

He'd tugged out an all-black, one-piece activity suit which he covered with a light blue coat. He'd employ the hood on the suit later, when it was needed. For now, he was simply grateful he'd had the forethought to pack this jacket. He added a pair of glasses, ones that obscured some of his face, hoping that anyone looking wouldn't be discerning. Thankfully, his time with the designates had been minimal while aboard the Captivar, so he hoped they wouldn't recognise him with this outfit.

The bathroom door opened, and Nala came out. Her outfit was more modern than anything she'd worn before. A skirt and top in vivid green. It didn't quite mould to her body but came close, outlining her curves. It was teamed with knee-length boots of silver and white. She'd tossed her hair into an updo, which displayed her slender neck, and he felt the rise of his body once again.

"Do I look fast?" she asked.

He blinked at her query. "Fast?"

"You know, inappropriate. Unladylike." She licked her lips, and he had to restrain the groan that rose.

"Not at all. You look… amazing." Oh, and didn't she just! She looked like a siren, and his body responded to that knowledge.

She gave an uncertain laugh. "I feel exposed in this outfit, but looking at what people around me are wearing, I don't want to stand out too much, and after some of the comments today, I feel I need to make more of an effort to dress for the times." Her hands fiddled before her.

"You look fantastic, and their comments were inappropriate. You're acclimating in a fashion you're comfortable with. That's all that matters. Now, you have a wet weather coat?"

She held it up, showing him the full-length grey coat of wool, and he nodded.

"Remember, your safety is paramount. If you feel any threat, remove yourself from the situation, and I'll move in."

His guts curdled at the thought of her being endangered, but there was nothing more they could do. They needed information, and so far, they'd not found enough to give them a boost in their investigation.

Nala walked to the door. "We should head out now," she said, and her hand rested on the button.

"Wait!" Alric hurried to her, grabbed her shoulder, and spun her so she faced him. "Nala, I don't want you to get hurt." His words weren't sufficient, hell, he needed to let her know how important she was to him.

He dragged her against him, knew his breath fanned her face, and couldn't miss the startlement in her eyes.

His lips crashed down on hers, needing to infuse the moment with the depths of his fears. She could be seriously hurt if the person behind the attacks saw her as a threat.

Their mouths clung, and he tasted her, the sweet honey of her, and revelled in the delicious press of her curves against him.

He knew time was melting away, but he increased the pressure for another moment then tugged away. Cupped her cheek as his gaze roamed over the soft pink flesh. "Stay safe, Nala. We have a lot to discover, and I refuse to lose you before we can sort this out," he growled.

She smiled, it was wobbly, and terror flashed quickly before dying away. It was like a punch to his gut, and he had to steel himself to withstand that impact.

"I will, Alric, I promise. And yes, we do have lots to explore."

Stepping back was the most difficult thing he'd ever done. Letting her go was like physically carving off a body part, but it was necessary. At least, within the hotel she was reasonably secure, but outside was a different kind of beast.

He released her, told her to give him a two-minute head start, and he pushed past her, heading for the stairs. Moving quickly, he descended to the ground floor and held the door open but stayed within the shadows of the potted plants. The only hint of green in this city. His sour thought filled the moment until the ding of the elevator stole his attention, and there she was stepping off and into the lobby.

Scanning the area, he relaxed when he noted that no one had moved or appeared to be interested in her as she strode out of the building.

He followed, staying as unobtrusive as possible. When she crossed the road, he scanned the crowd and cursed, moving faster so he could remain close enough to act if necessary. When Nala lifted the communicator to check the direction, he slowed slightly, so he wouldn't appear out of the ordinary. She turned right and he moved in the same direction, touching his hand to the small earpiece he wore, as if listening to a conversation.

At the restaurant, she stilled, her hand on the door, and he inhaled, aware she was nervous. She entered, and he moved past the door, slid into the small alleyway, and divested himself of the coat he wore over his suit. Lifted the hood to cover his hair and shoved the coat into the backpack he'd dragged from his pocket. Whipping the glasses off, he shoved them into the bag as well and hoped that was enough of a change to make him less obvious.

Nala saw Alric enter in the window reflection, even though she was careful to keep her gaze averted while ordering a drink.

"It's so good you could attend," Sarah said, grabbing her hand and patting it. "We heard about Gwendolyn and…" She turned away and Nala felt awkward.

"I…" Nala didn't get a chance to finish.

"Why were you sent to a different location?" a woman Nala knew as Heather, enquired.

The pilots both stared at her. "Why were you sent with the captain and not either of us?"

Nala shook her head. "I don't… I think it had something to do with when we were first boarded," she said, unsure how much to share.

"There's been accidents, and we're all terrified," Heather added, and Nala nodded.

"I heard about them. Sarah told me about Gwendolyn and… Is there any news?" She scooted forward on her seat, aware that the latest was Gwendolyn would survive but was now under guard. No one in or out until she was able to regain consciousness and tell them what happened.

Sarah shook her head. "They won't tell me, just that she's critical but stable, whatever that means." She stared at Nala. "You'd know, wouldn't you? It's a medical term."

The coffees arrived and Nala breathed a momentary sigh of relief. How do I answer? If this wasn't so furtive, she would have asked Alric, but he was slouched in a corner booth, pretending to be a student. Close enough to help if necessary, but discreet enough in his disguise that if he wasn't needed, he'd remain out of their area of interest.

The group murmured among themselves as the drinks were circulated, and Nala took a deep swallow, hoping it would give her courage. Eventually the group looked back in her direction. "I… When they say stable, it means that the body is equalised and the vital signs are within normal parameters even though her injuries are bad, which is the critical aspect. They are dealing with the items that are not in normal condition."

"That's not very clear," Heather whined.

"No, it really doesn't tell you much, but these terms are vague for a reason," Nala pointed out. "There's not just a duty of care, there's also a duty and right to privacy, which all doctors and nurses subscribe to. I doubt that has changed much since I was a nurse."

Sarah nodded. "Tonight's just a quick meet-up, so I can walk you back to the hotel, if you'd like. We could catch up?"

Nala heard the hopeful note, but her brain spun quickly. "I'm actually really tired, Sarah. We could catch up tomorrow?"

The woman stared at her, and Nala discerned something in her gaze.

Nala grew cold and a defensive itch started at the base of her skull.

"Of course," Sarah responded, and Nala breathed out, almost laughing when she considered how irrational her reaction was.

All this cloak-and-dagger is affecting my thinking processes.

As the coffees and other beverages were finished, members of the group rose and drifted away with cries of "see you in a few days," and "thanks, everyone."

The group left was small, intimate, and Nala realised it was time to leave. She rose, checking to ensure her communicator was safely in her pocket, and smiled at Sarah. "I should head back to the hotel. I need to check in with my mentor."

"I could walk you over, and we can talk on the way," Sarah said.

Even though Nala couldn't come up with a reasonable excuse, she didn't want Sarah to walk with her, because she hoped that once she returned to hotel, she and Alric might have an opportunity to talk.

"Oh, I'll be fine on my own," Nala said. "We can catch up later, if you'd like though? Tomorrow is fine?"

"Of course," Sarah answered, though Nala detected this didn't quite meet with her agreement.

With a quick wave, Nala hurried through the door and headed along the pavement at a rapid clip. Her nerves quivered, because she knew this was the logical time when an attack might be made.

A sound captured her attention, and she looked over her shoulder but didn't see anyone. That unnerved her further, and she sped up, noting for the first time that the roads were quiet, with few vehicles, lights shining coming toward her.

As she turned back something pushed her.

Lights whirled in a kaleidoscope as she fell, the road rising to meet her while she screamed, trying to aim herself toward the kerb.

Her hands scraped as she connected with the asphalt, knees throbbing as honking filled the air. Any second and it will all be over. She sobbed and tried to rise.

Hands grabbed her, tugging her up.

Water splashed up, soaking her.

The beating of a heart, heat from a hard body, impinged on the darkness. Strong arms circled her as she shook, not sure her legs would hold her.

"I nearly didn't get here in time," Alric muttered, holding her close. "I was close by, but still not close enough."

Nala squeezed her eyes shut as the adrenaline started to crash. "Let's get out of here," she groaned.

He swung her up, into his arms.

"I can walk," she whispered against his chest.

"Maybe you can, but I need to feel you alive. So don't complain."

Nala sighed, slid her hands around his neck, and let the sense of safety wash over her.

17

Alric eased Nala down onto the bed, noting the raw scrapes and bruises on her knees. "Stay here," he ordered, and Nala nodded.

In the bathroom, he'd stashed his emergency medical kit. He grabbed it and rooted through it, looking for anti-microbial and viral swabs to clear away any debris which may have become embedded. Then he found a medicated cream to assist with the healing. Lastly, the skin replacement patches joined the other items. He would apply them to keep the newly cleaned wound areas sanitary while they healed.

Nala was still shaking, sitting on the edge of the bed, and he cursed, because fury was coursing hard and hot through his veins. He'd seen the culprit, knew who it was, and he'd tell her after he'd attended to the most pressing task.

"You'll need to lose the skirt and top," he muttered.

Nala blanched. "What?"

He felt like a snake requesting that she all but strip, but the fit would make it difficult for her to remove once he'd applied the healing salves and skin cover. "I'll help you." He tried to avoid her gaze; her pupils too large as she stared at him.

"I…"

"I promise not to take advantage," he growled.

Under other circumstances, the blush on Nala's cheeks would have entranced him, and the opportunity to see her in only her underthings would have filled him with lust, but right now she needed his care and attention.

"But Alric…"

"Think of me as your doctor. You'd…"

Nala shook her head at his words. "No, only the nurse would have done that," she muttered.

"Okay then. Your nurse."

"Only women, Alric."

He gritted his teeth. "We need to get you out of the skirt and shirt. Once I apply this, they will be in the way, and you won't be able to do it alone with those scraped hands."

"Oh, uh, yes."

He took her chin between his thumb and fingers. "I won't take advantage, Nala. So please, let me help you out of them."

She bit her lip and gave a short nod, but in her eyes, there was a sheen of angry tears as she stood and turned.

He found the clips holding the blouse in place along the neck of her top and released them, then carefully slid the sleeves down. Miles of creamy flesh was exposed, and his knees shook as he followed the same process with her skirt, sliding the zip on the side down, and she stepped free. He didn't miss the way her knees wobbled too.

Once he'd laid her clothes on the chair, he returned and kneeled before her. His gaze roamed over the injuries. Thankfully, they wouldn't need extensive care, just a clean and cream. He gently took the swab and wiped it over the injury.

"Ow," she moaned.

"Sorry," he muttered.

He carefully swiped the mess, ensuring he'd get it cleaned up without any further pain. He dabbed the cream onto the tip of his finger and smeared it over the wound, before applying the skin replacement patch, then moved to the other leg, repeating the process.

He glanced at the area around the injury, and on impulse, he leaned in and kissed above the first then the second injury. "My mother used to kiss my hurts away," he whispered, reaching for her hand.

The wounds there were deeper, a gash bleeding fitfully. Grabbing a fresh set of swabs, he once more set to work, cleaning, swiping, then applying the skin cover.

"Now to kiss that better too." His lips found the warmth of her skin, needing to infuse the caress with all the emotions that roiled inside him.

He rose and disposed of the used swabs, the packets that had contained the skin replacement bandages, and put the cream away before returning to her.

Nala watched him in silence, and now he saw the lacy underwear she wore. He gulped, aware that he was seeing far more of her flesh than he'd expected. *She's injured, you barsha fool.*

She wound her arms around the cups of her bra. "Alric?"

He waited for her to speak, tongue-tied but hungry. He reined in his lust and stepped close. "What can I do for you, Nala?"

She blinked. "I nearly died tonight. I... I would have died a virgin. I'd never know what it feels like to be held, loved." She spoke so softly he had to lean in to hear her words.

Any answer that rose was strangled before it could emerge. Heaven knew he wanted her. His emotions ran deep, but he wasn't going to take advantage of her in a moment of weakness.

"Alric? You don't want me?" She asked, her long lashes framing eyes that oozed pain and embarrassment.

He winced. "I do, Nala. I want you so much I ache morning and night. But you're hurt, and the emotions you feel in response are blinding you. I know you feel like you could have missed something important, but you deserve..." He paused. "We deserve something that isn't furtive or rushed. When we make love—and I have no doubt we will—I want it to be because we both desire it. Not because you've had a terrible experience that causes your body to tell you what you need. Sex is an emotional connection. It's..." He snaked a shaking hand through his hair. "It marks you for life. Nothing you can see, but deep inside you. You'll always remember your first time."

Her lips trembled. "You won't...?"

He shook his head and pulled her into his embrace. "When or if we make love, it will be because it's a time and place of our choice."

"Oh," she whispered, and she folded in on herself, as if she were deflating in his arms. She'd overcome so much, and he hated to think that he'd been the one to let her down and leave her so dejected.

"Come on, love. You need to get into your pyjamas, and I'll order food for us. Then you'll crawl into bed and sleep. I'll be here, watching out for you."

"Okay," she whispered and pulled away from his arms.

He sighed and watched as she gathered the clothing and disappeared into the bathroom, while he ordered food, looking for things he felt she'd like best. Then he considered what he'd learned tonight, and replayed the attack in his mind, which chilled his blood.

Now that he knew who the attacker was, they had to come up with a plan. Something he'd discuss with Nala later. Once the first flash of emotion had passed, he was sure they'd be able to track them down.

Then they could make plans.

Nala woke early, aware that Alric's arms surrounded her, kept her close and safe.

Revisiting the attack from last night was horrific. Of all the things she'd faced—being thrust through time, the loss of her identity, past and future—this was the one scenario that terrified her.

Sliding from the bed in silence, she padded to the window, raised the blinds just enough that she could see a sliver of daylight, and gazed out onto the road. The buildings were alien, monoliths of glass and steel. The hivelike structures rising stories into the air, too tall to see the tips above the clouds. Nothing like that had existed in her time.

Vehicles growled their away along snarled roads, and those soaring above the air whizzed past at speeds that made her dizzy.

So much had changed. She'd thought England had changed since the war when she was last there. But everywhere had. Places she knew felt like it was another planet when she'd seen the changes after travelling through the wormhole.

"Are you okay?" Alric's quiet inquiry broke through her thoughts.

"Did I wake you?" She dropped the blind back down and turned to him.

"No, I think I was waking anyway. How do you feel?"

Her knees and hands still stung, but she smiled. "Fine. I was just…" She shrugged. "I didn't want to wake you."

"I don't suppose you'd like to come back so I can say good morning properly?" He twitched his brows in a comical fashion, and she giggled.

"I might be able to be persuaded," she said with a laugh.

"Talk, talk, talk," he answered and winked, and she headed toward him. Even as she crawled onto the bed, he was reaching for her.

As their lips met, the fire that banked inside her built, searing her from the inside out. When they parted, his brow rested against hers, and her chest moved like the bellows the blacksmith down the road from her childhood had used.

"Alric?"

"Yes, love?"

"I want you. I want this to be my first time." And she did. Knowing the mechanics of intercourse, she'd never been tempted. No other man had seemed the right choice to give up a future where she was in control.

His fingers dug deep. "Tonight then, we'll make plans."

She blinked. "I… I need to know about some things though. I mean, in my time, there weren't precautions… Or at least, not for women, but I saw some information…" Heat burned the skin of her face and she made to tug away.

"Don't be embarrassed, love. Choosing to share your body is one thing, choosing to grow a child, another. There are choices we can take." He cupped her cheek. "We both share responsibility, and as you've already had the medical testing, we can arrange for a short-term blocker if you wish. I too will protect you. Condoms, or sheaths, are widely available."

"Oh, back in my time, they were… They weren't acceptable, except for married couples, and even then…" She shrugged, because explaining that things were taboo when they were clearly now considered normal was difficult to accept.

"You can see a medical specialist if you like, remotely. If the hypospray option isn't available, we can go to a nearby clinic."

The deep-seated sense of shame spread through her, but she inhaled deeply, pushing it aside. "A remote appointment might be best," she muttered.

"Alright. I can arrange that immediately, and if you'd prefer, I can use the bathing room while you talk with the doctor."

He was giving her privacy, and she gratefully accepted it. "That… Yes, please."

Taking up her communicator, Alric had her open it up with her thumb, then he pressed the medical call application and scrolled through the options until 'prophylactic assistance' appeared on the screen. Handing it back without a word, he rose, and she watched as he left the room.

The consultation was handled quickly, and though she was sure she blushed and stammered like a fool, she had her prescription delivered to the device within minutes.

"Remember, you should attend the clinic within six months of beginning sexual activities for a thorough checkup," the doctor said, after having given her a brief rundown of the medical reasons this was necessary.

Nala nodded at the woman on the screen before it went dark.

"I'm really ready," Nala told herself.

Tonight.

Stalking to the bathroom door, she knocked three times. "Alric?"

He opened it, his eyes searching her face. "What do we need to do?"

"I have a prescription. I need to…" Once more at a loss, she waited for him to understand what she didn't and couldn't say.

"Alright, let me change and we'll have breakfast, then make arrangements to collect the spray."

She nodded, and just like that, the conversation was done.

Alric settled into the seat opposite Nala, glad he'd chosen the restaurant because the intimacy of the room was too… well, intimate.

"What do you remember from last night?" he asked her.

She squinted. "Hands pushing me, I saw the lights." She scrubbed her hands over her face, and though he wanted to lift them away, he waited for her to find her equilibrium.

"Do you know who…?" Tricky ground here, he knew.

"I… No. Did you see?"

He gave a slow nod, watching her face the entire time. "I saw her."

Nala stiffened. "Her?"

"It was Sarah. She pushed you. I caught a glimpse of her face. Fury and a cold glint in her eyes. It was intentional," he added, needing Nala to understand the truth.

"But she's my friend," she breathed. "I… I trust her. So does Gwendolyn."

"Which is what makes this situation even worse. I notified the hospital to ensure no one that isn't a registered medical assistant has access to Gwendolyn. She's protected, but as for the rest…" He shrugged.

"You checked Sarah's apartment?" Nala's eyes didn't leave his face. She supposed they would need to see if she was there, or had left any clues.

"I sent someone last night, after you were asleep. I let Eshant know, and he has men monitoring the building, but she didn't return last night."

Nala opened her mouth, but he shook his head. "Here's breakfast," he said as the waiter returned with a tray. The fruits and baked goods were settled on the table, and only when the man left, did Alric breathe a sigh of relief. "I did consider sending a bulletin to the rest of your designate group, then discounted it. The truth is, if someone is hiding her, the last thing we need to do is alert her."

"So, what do we do now?" Nala waited as he poured them each a juice from the carafe.

"Eshant is arranging a full interrogation of any records relating to her, and we'll be sending people to interview the rest of the designates, to see where she's hiding, if it's with one of the others or what they know. If not, we'll remind them not to divulge what they know either with each other or with her, if there's any contact."

"Well, that's all fine and good," Nala muttered, "but that doesn't tell us—"

"Gwendolyn woke while you were having your consultation with the doctor. We need to go see her, see what she can tell us. Maybe she knows where Sarah is, or who she's spent time with."

"She's... Sarah's a social butterfly. If there's someone who'd have an interest in..." Nala looked at him. "But I don't understand why she'd do it. There must be more to it."

Alric patted her on the hand. "Sometimes there's nothing other than they do. Some people are just born without the necessary emotional balance to understand what is okay and what isn't."

She fired up before his gaze. "This isn't about what's okay and what isn't. She wiped at least one person from the planet. She killed them." Nala's voice was filled with fury. "No one has the right to do that."

"No," he answered, entranced by the fire in her eyes.

"So, we need to find Sarah," she muttered.

"And find out as much about her as we can, so we can formulate a way to deal with her effectively, without endangering anyone. To do that, we need to know her motivator. Power, greed..."

"Okay. Eat first, then what?"

"Prescription, then we have a meeting."

"With Gwendolyn?" Nala asked.

"With Gwendolyn," he agreed.

18

Nala entered the hospital with Alric, aware the whole time that he was looking for Sarah. But would she really come here? Nala didn't know the answer, only that there was a risk; that given Sarah had been prepared to kill both Gwendolyn and her, that she'd have another try.

Even as she opened her mouth to ask, Alric shook his head. "Not now, my love. Later." He ushered her in through the doorway and headed for the elevator.

Her discomfort grew in the tiny box full of other people as they moved upward.

"You know where we're going?" Nala queried.

"Yes, I made enquiries and arranged for an escort when we reach the floor," Alric answered as the doors slid open and they stepped off. He led her around the corner then a second and third. "This way," he muttered and tugged her toward two older women who loitered.

"Captain," the younger of the two spoke, though 'younger' was maybe not quite the correct word. They were dressed in black dresses, of a traditional cut, if she remembered the way Sunny talked about the clothing style. The women looked like they were a hundred years old, yet they were spry, and their eyes had her wondering if they were younger. "This way," the woman muttered and led them up a corridor.

At a door, with a remote mechanism, they stopped. The older of the women whipped out a pass and the doors slid open. "Quickly," she said and herded them inside just in time to see it close with a snap.

The older woman slid her hand up her throat. "Come this way," she said and peeled off a mask to reveal a much-younger woman, before removing a set of sleeves that also covered her hands. "A very useful way to conceal who you are and how old," she said, smiling at Nala. "I take it you're the designate leader, Nala Stimson?"

Nala nodded, still awestruck by the change, and watched as the second woman followed suit so two much-younger women stood before her.

"These are my security experts, Officer Landra Brian and Major F'nar Elphinstone. Both are highly decorated and were tasked with ensuring Gwendolyn's safety." When Alric turned to enquire, "What is her condition?" Nala welcomed the moment. Never in her existence had she seen anything like the prosthetics both women had worn like a second skin. If they'd had the likes of these, then it would have made a tremendous difference to the many men and women who still suffered from the war. Back in your time, her brain added. It seemed like anything was possible now.

"Nala?" Alric's voice broke through her reverie.

"I'm sorry. I was just…" She waved a hand, searching for the words to describe what she was seeing.

"You're from the ancient past, of course," said F'nar. "A lot of this assistance is old by our standards, but hadn't been invented when you lived." The words were spoken with a kindness, yet it once again reminded Nala that much had changed and she had a lot to learn and catch up on.

During the time she'd got lost in her thoughts, then during F'nar's words, they'd travelled the length of a corridor. Two burly men waited outside a door, and when they arrived, the men moved aside.

They were met by a third man when they stepped inside the room.

"Captain, Officer, Major, Designate. You've come to talk to the designate, Gwendolyn McCarty?"

Alric nodded. "We'll need everyone to vacate the room except myself and Nala."

The man's eyes narrowed. "If you insist." Though clearly, he wasn't at all happy with the idea that his presence was unnecessary and unwanted.

"I do," Alric answered, and they waited in silence until the three left and the door closed.

Alric brushed aside a curtain and there lay Gwendolyn, face pale and her body encased in a metal tube.

Nala reached out, but was restrained by Alric. "You mustn't touch the screens or the tube surrounding her."

Nala wasn't sure why but there was a gruffness in his voice. "Okay," she replied, and he released her. She crept forward. "Gwendolyn?"

"Nala," she breathed. Her eyes opened halfway in a swollen and battered face. She licked her lips. "They tell me I'm lucky. I broke my spine and both legs. My pelvis too." Tears dribbled down Gwendolyn's face as she gasped, obviously in pain. A beep echoed then a near-silent woosh.

Nala watched as the lines of pain drained away from her face.

"That's an anaesthetic. The tube is monitoring for signs of stress, and provides the necessary environment to ensure her bones knit optimally," Alric informed her.

"But her spine," Nala whispered. She knew well that meant quadra- or paraplegia, depending on the location.

Her fingers itched to touch Gwendolyn, to soothe away the pain, but Alric's warning echoed in her mind.

"Gwendolyn, we won't keep you, but we need to ask some questions." Alric pulled up two chairs, urging Nala to settle in one. "Did you see who did this?"

"I... Yes," Gwendolyn muttered. "It was Sarah. She said I stood in her way."

"What do you mean?" Nala frowned. "She's... You all have the same privileges and opportunities."

"Not according to her. She was angry because she saw you and him meeting me. Said I was siding with the enemy, just like before." Gwendolyn spoke slowly, her eyes glazed.

"Is she or can you discern if she's made contact with any of the other designates in a way that seems odd or different?" Alric pressed, and Nala wondered why he would ask that.

"No," Gwendolyn answered. "I know she and the co-pilot were friendly too, I can't say if it was more... sexual. You know." She blushed. "He and she used to disappear from the group before our placement, and I guess they kept in touch..."

"Why do you say that?" Nala asked.

"They were always the first to arrive. Like they were... Like they were a couple," Gwendolyn clarified. "No one said anything, because you know of the moral and professional implications, Nala. I think most of us guessed that there was something there. He wasn't married and neither was she. And that rock she carried on a chain..." Gwendolyn sucked in a breath. "What's going to happen to me, captain?"

Alric sighed. "The prognosis is good. The spinal break wasn't as traumatic as first expected. This repair tube will be injecting your body with medical nano-probes, which will be working to fuse the breaks. They'll be checking the spinal cord, and if necessary, assisting the body to repair itself."

"Will I walk again?"

Nala inhaled. If she could... What an amazing feat of medical technology if that was the case. Had medical care moved on to that extent? Was it possible the body could repair, what in her time, was a total disability?

"I don't know, and I can't say if the doctors are sure you'll be able to walk unaided again, that depends on many factors, but if it can be done, the nano-techs will be making every attempt to fully rehabilitate your body."

Alric reached over and squeezed Nala's hand as if he understood her thoughts.

He rose and helped Nala up, before asking, "If she was staying with the co-pilot, do you know…"

"She wouldn't stay with him. In the hallway, before she pushed me, she made it clear he was a means to an end."

Alric swore, and Nala leaned toward Sarah, to whisper in horror, "Do you think she'd hurt him?"

"I didn't think she'd do this to me, but here I am, looking at a ceiling." Gwendolyn spoke drily then coughed. "Oh Lord, that hurt," she moaned.

"We'll go and leave you. You have guards, and when you're healed, Nala and I will—"

"Together, are you? That was quick, Nala."

She bit her lip at Gwendolyn's words. There was no malice, but her own sense of morality was warning her that she'd rushed her agreement with Alric. Her chest ached and her guts churned.

"Nala?" Alric touched her hand. "We should go and let Gwendolyn rest."

"Oh yes, of course," she muttered. "I'll be back to check on you."

"Thank you for visiting," Gwendolyn said and closed her eyes.

Alric ushered Nala from the room, aware that those waiting outside wanted to know exactly what was said. He had no intention of sharing though. They didn't need to know the details of the investigations.

"No one in and out who is not a registered care provider from the hospital. Eshant will give you the details you require. In the meantime, continue the security protocols as set in place. If you have concerns, contact me."

They moved away, and Alric tightened his grip on Nala's hand. "That was hard for you."

She shuddered, and once they were around the corner, he stopped Nala and tugged her into his arms.

"She…" Nala shook her head. "I don't know how to process all this. So much has changed, and I don't know where I belong," she muttered.

"With me, right now," Alric told her.

"But is it right?"

He knew what she meant by the anguish in her voice, and if he let it, it may yet break him. "You think we're rushing this? We can wait, if you're not yet ready, Nala. Nothing is set in stone." Though it suddenly felt like one had lodged in his gut.

"I'm… I'm out of my depth, Alric. Things that were said and done. The tube with the nanotechnology, and the suits your officers wore. It's the constant reminder that I'm out of time and out of place. I don't belong here." A touch of hysteria edged in her voice.

"Nala, stop it. You can't change what is, and neither can I. I'm here to help you. Guide you. But you need to understand that we can't do this alone. We must find Sarah before anyone else dies."

Nala stilled under his hand, and he felt the contraction of muscles before she nodded, the movement jerky. "Yes, of course, captain."

It hit him hard that she called him 'captain' instead of Alric. He was a man, and one in over his head with the woman before him.

He also didn't miss the frost which tinged her words, and he wondered if he'd been too harsh, but Nala was… His brain searched for the right word. 'Sensible' hardly covered it. She'd been in a sort of controlled acceptance since the time he'd stepped onto the plane.

"Nala, I'm sorry. I wish we weren't dealing with this. I wish we…" He cupped her cheek and forced her to look him in the eyes, willing her to understand he empathised. "In normal circumstances we'd have time and space to get to know each other, but Gwendolyn's alive and we need to make sure the rest of the passengers are too. We don't have time for—"

She slid down the wall to the floor, pulling her legs close to her body and her hands over her face. "I'm so sorry, Alric. I'm… I feel like I'm fracturing, and I don't know who and what I am anymore. I thought Sarah was my friend, and my other friend Gwendolyn is in a hospital, and we don't know if she'll walk again, and my brain is over-loaded because so much has changed!"

Nala sniffled, and he crouched in front of her. "I think that's the first time you've cried, Nala. You've been so stoic, and I think…"

He scooped up a tear on his finger and gazed at it, aware that he had never seen her fall apart. There had been no strong emotions many might exhibit after the kinds of traumatic changes she'd experienced from her since they'd travelled through time. Even on the ship, when she'd been using her own body to cover and protect the others, she'd been terrified but also protective of others. He'd almost forgotten she too had lost everything. He needed to remind himself she'd also suffered like the others.

"You've lost so much, and not once have you screamed or raged. I couldn't manage that." He admired the strength of character which had kept her on her feet. In all honesty, he doubted he'd have coped so well under the circumstances.

"I lived through the blitz. When everyone around you is in danger, when night after night houses around yours are destroyed by fire and bombs, there's little else to do." She swiped at her eyes. "I survived when lots of others didn't, and this time, I'll do the same. I just need to catch my breath."

He heard the words, and in his mind, he saw a very young girl sitting in the ruins, looking at the sky and wondering why she'd survived when others didn't. It almost broke his heart that the girl had grown up to lose everything all over again.

"I'm sorry this happened to you. I do take responsibility for my part, but Nala, I want to help you. If what's between us is too much for you, then tell me now. I can step back until you're ready." He waited, his nerves quivering while he watched her.

"I don't want that, Alric." She inhaled, nostrils flaring. "What is between us, it could be fleeting or something more. You're my anchor, Alric. I just… Yes, it's hard right now, and I'm… Oh Lord, I'm having a moment. I'm sorry." She pushed up and he followed her.

"Nala, you don't need to hide—"

Her chin tightened. "I'm not hiding. I just needed a moment, and now it's passed." He watched as she inhaled, closed her eyes for a second, and when she reopened them, her gaze was clear. "So, what next?" she asked.

Alric wasn't sure he liked her tone or change in demeanour, but he had to accept it, because she clearly knew what she wanted.

"We need to go see the co-pilot and maybe his mentor. See what they know and find out if Sarah's been staying there or given any indication to where she might be holed up."

Nala nodded. "Then we should go." She stepped forward, but he reached out, tugged her back. For a moment, their eyes met, hers wide with surprise at the unspoken words, then she blinked. "Later. But for now, it's time to go."

The trip to the mentor was swift, and he'd already considered the questioning he'd need to employ, so when the woman opened the door, he was ready.

"Simmons, we need to talk to you about Sarah."

Her face hardened, and he got the impression that she was unsurprised that he'd arrived at her door. "Come in, captain. Uh, sorry, I don't remember your name," she said to Nala.

"Nala. Nala Stimson," she answered, but he felt her stiffness and shoved his hands into his pockets.

"Tell me about Sarah," he demanded, and the woman offered them a seat, and they settled onto the sofa in front of Simmons.

"Captain, she only stayed here the minimum week, saying she'd rather find her own place and way, but during that time I found her to be furtive. Secretive. She would spend hours undertaking the virtual lessons. She exhibited an interest in computing almost immediately, and I assisted her to access further learnings in this area."

The delivery of the information was spare, rote even, and he knew much of it came from practice with handling designates, having had two previously. The crewmember from the Captivar was also a capable computing technician. In this instance, she'd have been the pair of choice because of her technical ability.

"What else do you remember?" He leaned forward in his seat.

"She liked to watch the mass transit and street level cams. Particularly of specific neighbourhoods. I had the impression she was looking for a home base, I guess. Captain, is she connected to the deaths of designates?"

He stared at Simmons. "What do you know about them?"

"Only chatter on the blind channels. No one has specifics, but these sorts of things get out eventually," the woman answered.

Nala remained silent but tense beside him, and he wondered what she thought, until she spoke softly. "Did she leave anything behind?"

Simmons shook her head. "Nothing, but you can check the room if you'd like."

Nala hated that she'd lost control of her emotions. Since childhood, that control had been important to her. It was how she'd dealt with the war, her father's absence, and the devastation which surrounded her night after night. Now, Alric had seen the weakness she hid from everyone else. The one she refused to admit to.

What was it about Alric that caused her to let go of the restraints she'd held onto for so long? Even as she'd struggled with the truth that someone she'd considered a friend was a murderer, and that Gwendolyn had been physically impacted, he'd been there, and had been a strength she could call on. She'd been able to let go. With so much spiralling in her brain, she had to pick out the major issues to address.

She sat next to Alric on the mass transit system after they'd visited Simmons, and tried to make head from tails of what was going on.

"She spoke of the blind channels. What was that?"

He grunted. "I'll explain later, but not here or now. It's not secure."

She nodded her agreement and thought about the meeting they'd just had. Alric was right that she had to be clear about what she wanted emotionally, and that they needed to find the key to Sarah's whereabouts, but that was the least of their problems.

"Nala," he spoke softly, touching her on the hand. "Our stop is next."

"Oh," she murmured and stood along with him, making her way to the door. "I didn't realise."

"You were lost in your own thoughts."

She nodded. "You're right. I had to consider what happened earlier today, so I could concentrate on the next task."

The door opened and they stepped out. "We need to go this way." He nodded to the left, and they climbed the stairs and headed for the muted sunlight.

At the top, they stopped. "Oh my," she breathed, glancing up to the tops of the buildings.

"It's great to visit, but could you live here?" His question had her turning toward him.

"I... I think you're right. No, I don't want to live here. I like the green and open spaces. London before the war was cold and dark, and a little like this. No, I think you're right."

He smiled and her stomach turned in loops.

"We should get moving, love," he said, and they moved quickly, heading toward the crossing. "Nearly there," he called.

The building directly in front of them had a set of sliding doors, and as they entered, she heard a scream.

Alric sprinted across the foyer, and Nala followed, moving as quickly as she could.

A knot of people had gathered by the elevators, and he pushed through to the centre. "Damn, Nala! I need you now!"

Voices called out, "who are you?" and "what are you doing?"

"I'm Captain Alric Reys of the Captivar. I need someone to contact the NYLEO immediately."

The person beside the patient on the floor looked up, terror leaching the colour from their face. "I don't know..."

"Let me in," Nala whispered. "I know what's best in this situation."

The man kneeling beside the injured person shoved away, and Nala took his place, kneeling beside the pilot, whose blood had seeped out onto the polished marble floor. "Captain Michaels, can you hear me?"

"I... Yesss...." The sound was nearly inaudible. His eyes opened a crack.

"I need a pad," she called, her hand pushing down on the wound in his stomach, although she was aware that his chances of survival were slim. Someone shoved a jacket at her, and she took it, using it as a pad while pressing down hard, hoping to stem the pulsing liquid. She'd seen injuries like this before and knew the dangers. She checked his pulse, finding it thready.

"Was it Sarah?" Alric's demand cut through the air.

"Ye...eesss," the pilot answered.

"Do you know where's she's hiding?" Alric queried.

"Noooo...." Michaels whispered.

"I'm losing him," Nala muttered, watching the way his body was weakening, and the cold, clammy touch of his hand as he reached up, fingers sliding across the skin of her wrist.

"Na...la..." the pilot coughed, the sound faint, and his face screwed up.

"Damn," Alric muttered, looking up, and Nala looked at him.

"Alric?" she said, but something caught his attention and he rose and hurried away.

She remained beside the pilot, glancing back down, with a muttered imprecation. This wound is fatal, she thought, watching until the light left his eyes and his body stilled.

She slumped.

One more lost.

"He's dead," someone screamed as the medicals arrived on the scene, dragging bags.

A man crouched beside her, and she turned her head.

"It's too late," she whispered. "He expired as you were entering the building." She raised her hands to wipe away the tears, but the blood which coated them dripped down her arms.

19

Alric saw the furtive movements of the person on the edge of the crowd. He was sure it was Sarah, even though the individual wore a jacket with a hood. When the person looked up, his suspicion was confirmed. It was Sarah, and he caught sight of the flash of satisfaction that glinted in her eyes.

She sprinted away from the edges of the crowd as he pushed his way through, following her. The crowd held him up, so that once he was outside the building, he was scanning left and right to see which direction she'd gone.

Fury coursed through his veins. So close and yet out of reach. He'd lost the scent, and frustration ate at him.

His attention was splintered as the paramedics arrived, their boxes of equipment hauled from the back of the vehicle, and it reminded him that he'd left Nala behind, taking control of that situation.

Following the paramedics into the building, he felt like someone was watching, laughing at him. He'd seen the truth in Nala's face, that the pilot, Christian Michaels, couldn't possibly survive. Too much blood had been lost.

When Alric once more entered the area where Nala had been, the pilot's body was already being covered, and Nala was in a corner, being offered wipes and towels so she could cleanse herself of the blood.

He cursed silently as he noted the tracks of tears on her cheeks and the defeat in her eyes.

Surging forward, he was stilled by a law enforcement officer with a "Sorry, sir, but this is a restricted zone."

Fishing out his identification, he held it up. "That is the designate leader I'm mentoring, and I'm working for Eshant."

The officer's shoulders squared. "I see. Apologies, sir. What do you need?"

"The body removed as quickly as possible. We know who the perpetrator is, they were in the crowd initially and I chased them, but... they got away."

"You know the identity?" The officer's eyes gleamed.

"NTK," Alric muttered.

"Oh, of course."

Released from the wearisome task of answering questions, Alric moved to Nala.

"I couldn't save him. I didn't have the skills or..." She shook her head.

"With all due respect, ma'am," the medical hovering beside her said, "there wasn't much else you could do under the circumstances. You attempted to staunch the flow, and you gave comfort in his last moments. Most people here wouldn't know what to do. It's not some-thing they have experience of." The paramedic made some notations on the chart. "You took charge, according to those who were there, barked out the order for a pad, and applied pressure. Quick thinking is something we paramedics must have. Have you considered, since you're a designate, a future in—"

"That's enough for now," Alric growled, hackles fully engaged. "Nala? We should head back to the hotel." He turned to the male paramedic and smiled. "She was a nurse before the transportation. A damned good one, if what I saw is anything to base my assumptions on. She's already prepared her application for further training."

"Uh, yes, sir," the paramedic muttered, backing away.

Alric took Nala's hand and tugged her close, so she was encircled by his arm, and he slowly propelled her out of the building and into the sunshine.

"I need to bathe," she muttered, and he realised the clothing she wore was soaked in blood.

"I'll organise a private transport," he said and led her to a stone seat, settling her against his side, and contacted a private supplier.

Within moments a car had pulled up to the front of the building, where they waited, and Alric ushered her inside before climbing in next to her and giving directions. Then they were headed for the hotel, the trip quick though circuitous.

Silence wound itself around them, and once they had arrived, they made their way to the room.

He hated the impotence which surrounded her, and the look of pain and loss in her eyes.

"I should have saved him," she said finally.

"You heard what the paramedic said. You couldn't." His hands found her shoulders, and he stared hard at her. "You can't blame yourself for him dying. That was Sarah. She killed him, plunged the knife into his gut."

Her lower lip wobbled, and he groaned, ready to pull her into his arms.

"I'm covered in blood," she whispered. "I need to get clean."

Pulling away, Nala stalked to the bathroom door and entered the room. The door thudded behind her, and Alric sank to the bed.

He didn't need her to take on more pain, she'd already tried to shoulder the other death and injuries. Alric didn't know what or how to help her, and that sense of being helpless had him hanging his head, hands dangling between his legs.

The shower washed away the copper taint on her skin, but it didn't dispel the chill in Nala's soul. Another death, and Sarah was the culprit. She knew that. "I can't change the truth," she told herself as the spray of water, better than the sonic shower she'd had on the Captivar, ran down her body.

She'd allowed herself a moment to feel the loss of Michaels. Not that she'd known him well, but he'd been one of the members of her designate group. In those days when they'd been waiting for the mentor announcements, they'd mingled together, forming bonds with each other. Some more so than others, and she laughed, the sound discordant.

Snapping off the water, she stepped out, aware that the washing of her body allowed her also to cleanse away her guilt and disempowerment.

The drying system beckoned, but with a sigh she turned away in favour of one of the towels. She wrapped it around herself and stepped in the direction of the mirror.

Her eyes stared back at her, hazel with the green more dominant today, she supposed because of the green in the towel. Her hair, wet strands of dark, lay against her skin. Pale skin she'd hidden.

"Michaels is dead, but you aren't," she whispered. "You did what you were trained to do. You did what you could. No one asks for more."

In the back of her mind, she had a dim recollection of her grandmother, her face lined. She'd passed not long after the war began, and she'd been a canny woman, Nala guessed because she'd seen so much, especially in those long days in Kenya.

"Don't waste your life, my dove," she whispered to Nala.

Nala, the child, didn't really understand the imprecation of her grandmother but took the gnarled hand in hers.

"No, Grannie," she whispered. "I want to be a doctor."

"A fine vocation, dearie. Something good and strong. You'll make a difference."

Funny how that memory had flickered into her mind just when she needed it most. "Don't waste your life."

The importance of them wasn't lost on her now, when she personally had so much at stake. Alric… She bit her lip. How did she quantify the situation they found themselves in? Dangerous, yes, but more than that. She was motivated sexually and physically by his presence. Was it love though? She closed her eyes and let the towel drop to the floor. What would he see if she entered the bedroom nude?

She shivered at the thought, excited and petrified in equal order.

It's time, she told herself. Time to free herself from the constraints of a time she no longer belonged in.

Inhaling deeply once more, she let the oxygen fill her lungs, opened her eyes, and looked upon her body. Breasts like ripe melons, tipped with pert and jutting pink nipples. Her body lean.

It was time. She pulled away from the mirror, circled the doorknob with her hand and twisted it.

"Alric?"

"I'm here," he answered. The room was dim, and she breathed a sigh of relief then stepped into the room.

20

Nala's soft call had Alric turning in her direction. When the door opened and she stepped into the room, naked, he stilled.

She was simply the most alluring creature he'd ever seen.

Her body was finely moulded; long legs, flat belly, hips that flared gently, and her breasts mounds of pleasure tipped with ripe, strawberry-coloured nipples. He was… tongue-tied.

"Alric?"

His gaze found the trepidation on her face, the uncertainty in the way she held herself.

"Are you… Are you sure?" he said, fisting his hands and willing himself to remain where he was long enough for her to make the ultimate decision.

"I… Yes, if you want to."

The cravings inside him rose, clawing to get free. He took a step, then another, controlling his breathing and the rapid beat of his heart. "I do, love. But I want you to be sure."

She blinked. "I'm… I'm here and naked," she answered as her forehead crinkled.

Closing the distance between them, he let go of his restraint, his mouth dipping down to hers and devouring.

Her lips opened to him, not pliant but meeting his hunger surge for surge. Lips and tongues tangled, tested, and wanted more. His hands found the skin of her back, slid over the silken bounty, and roamed lower to find the roundness of her butt.

When his lips wandered to the curve of her cheek then down the length of her neck, she moaned and arched against him, and unable to restrain himself, he covered one of those precious mounds. Felt the jut of her nipple, and his body hardened further, cock pushing against his clothing.

"More. I want your skin against mine, Alric," she muttered.

He tugged away, noting the rosy hue on her skin, down her chest, and he smiled. "Anything you want, love."

His hands shook as he tore at his clothing, and they dropped to the floor, discarded and forgotten.

Her mouth formed an inciting smile, and she reached out. "May I touch?"

He shook, aware that she was a novice at this lovemaking, not that you'd know it by the way she slid her hand against his pectoral.

"Firm muscle mass," she said, before running the heel of her palm over his own distended nipple. "Very nice," and she leaned in to kiss him.

Her body rubbed against his, and heaven help him, his cock slid against her mound, the brush of hair electric and carnal.

He devoured her lips, needing so much more, as they danced their way to the soft bed, then his knees were against it, and they fell, bouncing as they landed on the mattress.

Dragging his lips away again, he inhaled deeply, letting the scent of her, all warm woman and arousal, curl around him. "Be sure, my love. Because I'm not sure I'll be able to pull away if you change your mind."

Her gaze met his, open. "I don't intend to. I want this and you. I want it now."

Inside Nala, there was a raging hunger, carnal and enticing. It urged her to throw off the last restraints as her body moved against his. He was hard yet soft, by equal degrees. His touch arousing but cautious, giving her time to accustom herself to the intimacy of their bodies entwined.

His kisses drugged while urging her to greater freedoms.

"I want to be with you, Alric. I need you to be my first."

His smile was tantalising. "It's a gift I'll accept then, with pleasure." His green eyes darkened yet sparkled with pleasure.

It warmed her, stoking the fire inside her, as his knee rose and rubbed gently against her mound. "Do you feel that, Nala?" he whispered.

"Oh yes," she moaned as the tender friction excited her further, and she was aware that her body was preparing itself for his entry, the dampness of her core coating him.

"Your body is readying itself, my love. You're wet and swollen—I can feel that."

His hand inched down her body, over her stomach, to find the thatch of hair that hid her most intimate parts. He touched her and she bucked against him, her breath catching.

"You're simply the most beautiful woman, my heart. Strong and tender, but giving. From the first moment I saw you, I wondered who the man would be who'd draw out the siren." His lips found the curve of her shoulder, and his tongue slid out to swipe at her. "You taste sweet, and I want it all. I want all of you, Nala. Every. Little. Bit."

His fingers slid between folds of skin to roll over the tiny pearl, and she cried out as pleasure arced through her, her body stiffening as he continued his assault.

"Inside you, warm and ready. So ready for me. Are you ready, my love? Do you want me to slide inside you and fill you up?"

The carnality of his words was both alien and drugging, and she wanted everything he said and more. She needed to be one with him, and in incoherent tones, she answered, "Inside me. I want you," while she panted and moaned.

"Then let me love you."

He rolled her, and she felt the whirl and the sudden pressure of his body over hers. Her breasts crushed against his chest. The zing of electricity made her move, widening her legs, and her hands found his back. Her fingernails bit deep into his flesh, while his mouth took hers in a bruising caress.

His body shifted once more so she felt his shaft nudging at her, demanding what she offered as he stilled momentarily. He lifted his head. "I love you, Nala."

Then he thrust, and it hurt. The rictus of pain radiating as she sucked in her breath. She knew of the pain, expected it, but still was unprepared for the moments where he held himself still, fully sheathed by her body. Her breath came in pants.

"It'll pass soon," he crooned, and she waited, anxious for the pleasure to return. She knew it would, because the few nurses who'd taken chances and lost their virginity had whispered of the experience.

Gradually, the pain subsided; the whole while Alric held himself tense, his face tight, mouth edged in white.

Then it was gone, and only the sensation of fullness remained. Her body wanted something, and she gave in, letting the pleasure take over. Her hips moved slightly, and the sensations were inexplicable. She gasped and he grunted.

"Nala?"

"Love me," she answered, knowing intrinsically he needed to hear her confirmation that the pain had passed.

His moves were gentle, alluring and intense. Each guaranteed to increase her pleasure, and she basked, while his hands slid over her skin before reaching her hips and gripping tight.

"Feel me," he muttered as the rhythm increased. He moved and she slid her legs around his hips, knowing only that her body demanded it, as her fingers twined in the sheets.

The assault on her senses increased. He thrust and withdrew, then thrust again, and each time inside her body the pressure grew and grew. It was as if a heated ball of need invaded her brain with arousal, and it tore away the ability to think.

She was lost in the maelstrom, hunger and insatiable need, until her last minuscule grip of reality splintered.

Her body stiffened, the orgasm wild and all-consuming, throwing her through the universe.

When she opened her eyes again, she watched him, his thrust ferocious and his face graven. His body heaving as he found his own release. Fingers held her still, brutally hard, digging into her flesh, but she welcomed it. She welcomed him.

He slumped, and she wound her arms around him, amazed that he shook, his body sweaty, and that he'd lost control with her.

Words couldn't convey just how beautiful the joining of their bodies had been, and as her mind was sluggish, she closed her eyes and let reality float away.

Alric held Nala in his arms and wondered at how she'd surprised him, both by the silent declaration and the ferocity of her lovemaking. He'd known she was a virgin, but the gift he'd been given was one he'd treasure, just as he'd treasure her.

He knew in his mind he wanted more than a single encounter or a season with Nala. He wanted it all, but he didn't ask for more, although the words of love had slipped from his mouth.

He hadn't meant to say them just yet, but he had, and he didn't regret it. If only he could be sure that one day she'd return them.

He pulled up the covers over their nakedness and closed his eyes, the sense of well-being in the moment dragging him under the depths of exhaustion.

21

Another fruitless day of search for Sarah. They'd checked her accommodation, and Nala had spoken with the last of the flight crew and other flight attendants. None seemed to know anything useful.

Back in the hotel room, she reclined on the seat, photo in hand. Nala studied the grainy image that Alric had thrust at her. He'd been in a meeting with the NYLEO while she'd been meeting with other designates, not that she'd been far from him, as he'd made the point that the inspectors needed to come to him.

"You're sure it was her?" Nala asked.

Alric nodded. "Absolutely. She was there, watching as you tried to save him."

Shaking her head, Nala considered the facts as she knew them about Sarah. She was in her thirties, though exactly how old, Nala was unsure. "She lived in Australia, she'd emigrated as an adult. She didn't talk about her parents, only that she'd made her own way in the world, and she had that necklace. The only time I asked about it, she was dismissive. She was furtive with it. She and Michaels were close. We, Gwendolyn and I, worked that much out. She spent time with him in his room. We did wonder if it was more than friendship, but, well, you didn't ask those kinds of questions or discuss anything except in a kind of innuendo, I guess." Squeezing her eyes shut, she said, "I do remember every now and again, there was a hint of something in her speech, like she didn't speak English as a first language."

Alric leaned forward. "Would you know it if you heard words or accents?"

Biting her lip, she considered. "Maybe. But I don't... Okay, we should try it."

She watched as Alric pulled up a list of countries on his communicator and requested ancient dialogue in languages. She didn't see which countries he had listed, but one by one, she listened. The fifth was it. "That one."

He frowned. "You're sure?" Alric seemed rather sceptical.

"Yes, why?"

He cleared his throat. "It's German."

She gasped and slumped in her seat. "You're absolutely sure?"

His nod reinforced the sense of betrayal that rose in her.

"The cow!" Her hand slid over her mouth. "I'm sorry, I shouldn't have said that aloud."

He laughed. "I've heard worse."

"But she hid who she was." It was a matter of honesty, and on that count, Sarah had failed. "I took her at her word," Nala fretted.

"Would it have done any good if you hadn't? What if you'd questioned her, what would you have asked?"

Considering Alric's words put the whole mess into a context she didn't want to examine. "I would have probably asked if she was a Nazi." Heat built inside her, but it wasn't like the heat she'd felt with Alric, it was a steaming lava flow. "She lied to all of us, hid the truth of what she was."

"She was an immigrant like you," Alric pointed out.

"Not like me. I was leaving behind a city ravaged by war."

"So was she," he said.

The horror ran too deep, her psyche scarred by memories of the war, the things she'd heard and the patients she'd seen after. Instead of being ready to consider what he was saying, she changed the subject. "What will you do with her when she's caught? What do you usually do with people like her, with tainted minds?"

He cocked his head. "Tainted minds?"

"You know, like a hysterical madness. We saw a lot of that in the years after the war."

"Is that what you called it?" He took her hand.

"One of many things, not that I spent much time in any of the psychiatric institutions, except during my training," Nala answered.

He shook his head. "Today we'd call it a form of psychosis. The underlying factors would be identified and a treatment plan devised."

"They used electric shock therapy, water treatment…"

His eyes were wide with surprise and something she hoped wasn't horror. "Oh God. No, today there's cognitive therapies, medication, surgical intervention if required. But we have so few issues, most of them are identified early on, in childhood or during the emergence."

"They can diagnose it that young?" She leaned forward. "That's extraordinary."

His smile was warm. "Much has changed in the medical field. The emphasis is on citizenship, ensuring everyone understands their responsibilities and from that comes rights."

She sighed. "Mental therapies were never really my area of interest. I wanted to help those who returned or were injured and disfigured by the war. The things we saw… I guess it impacted me more than I understood."

"I can't begin to understand what you experienced, Nala. But I want to be there as you learn and grow." When his hand enveloped hers, there was a sense of well-being.

She ran her thumb over the back of his hand. "I want that, Alric. I want to practice medicine and do good."

"Then we'd better find Sarah, so we can focus on giving you the life you want."

His words dimmed the glow that warmed her. "How?"

His gaze turned steady. "I have a plan. It's dangerous, but I think it will work."

The hair on the nape of her neck stood on end. "You want me to be bait again?"

He grunted. "I don't want that, but we need to find her and do it quickly."

Her guts knotted. "What if we could find her hole?"

"I'd prefer that, honestly. I don't want you endangered, but she's killed two, two are seriously injured, and she's already taken a pass at you. We need to conclude this game quickly, before she can strike again. The law enforcement officers found things of hers in Michaels's apartment."

"They checked? You already received a briefing?" He hadn't shared it, and that didn't sit well with her.

"Eshant sent me a quick report while you were in the bathroom, and I didn't want to spoil the mood." The way he smoothed down his clothing told her he was uncomfortable.

"If that wasn't the case, would you have shared the information?"

He rubbed a finger over his forehead. "Eventually. Nala, you were so upset with Michaels's death, I didn't want to make things worse." He shook his head and murmured, "We should order dinner to the room. That way we can talk in private."

"You don't want to continue this discussion in public?"

Alric appeared to stifle a laugh. "That and other factors." He raised his communicator, ordered a meal, and within minutes the meal was delivered, set up, and they were left. The conversation died away until they'd eaten their fill.

"You withheld the information," Nala said, strangely hurt by the omission.

He nodded. "From time to time, depending on what I learn, that is my job. As the captain of the Captivar, I make decisions about information. Much of which I can't share. It's my job and who I am, Nala. You have to understand that."

Closing her eyes now, she understood what he was saying. She couldn't take exception because, as he said, it was his job. When she opened her eyes, she reached back over and rubbed his hand. "I understand. I do. I shouldn't have questioned you on keeping it from me."

He smiled. "Are you finished?"

She glanced down at the remains of the meal on her plate and nodded. "Yes."

He tugged away his hand and stood, and she followed suit.

Morning came far too quickly for Alric. He stretched, feeling the warmth of Nala in the bed beside him. They hadn't made love again, although she'd shyly offered.

"You'll be too sore, my love. Come, sleep beside me, and in the morning, if you're not too uncomfortable, then I'm more than open to it." He grinned as she blushed, the red crest rising and once more intriguing him.

She shucked her clothing, though not without enticing glances below her lashes, and dashed beneath the covers.

He was aroused and aware that she knew it, but he forced himself to breathe slow and steady until the urgency of his need subsided to an ignorable level. Her body was soft and pliant next to his, and he pulled her close so he could inhale her scent and slide his arm around her waist.

When she drifted off, he'd been unable to sleep, aware that in the morning they would need to discuss his plan. Unless she thinks of anything that assists, he told himself, finally letting his eyes droop shut.

He woke suddenly, feeling her jerk awake beside him. "The ring," she uttered. "I know where I've seen it!"

"What do you mean?" He tried to hold her, but she wiggled against him until he released her.

"It's Russian. I'm sure of it. I remember when we went to the museum in Brisbane. They had these jewellery cases in there. It's… a Romanov ring. Or similar. The ring was big, so clear and white, and Mum said she'd never seen a diamond that clear before. Except the one Grannie had from their time in Africa. Mum told me at the time that Grandad and Grannie had gone to south Africa on business, he'd bought it then. But it was smaller, more like a chip, I guess. It was left to my brother Edmund for when he got married."

"So, Sarah likely has some association with Russia." But that didn't make sense in his mind. The little he knew was Germans and Russians had been on opposite sides of the conflict.

"The Russians were allied to Germany until they swapped sides," Nala said drily.

Alric had so little understanding of that time. "Wait, Sunny may have some information," he muttered.

Nala stared at him. "About what?"

"A lot of countries changed and morphed before, during, and after the war. Maybe we're missing something important."

"I have no idea what you mean," she muttered as he reached for the communicator.

"Uh, should I dress?" Nala whispered just before he could press the button, and he blushed.

"I can disengage the video screen," he said, and did so before pressing the button.

"Big brother, what do you want? I'm about to go to bed." Sunny's voice filled the room.

"Hello to you, sunshine. I need some information, and I think you can help. I need to know about the boundaries of Germany and Russia during and after World War II. Were brides and families from Russia brought to Germany?"

"Ha! Yes and no." Sunny spoke slowly, as if sifting through the information in her mind. "Most who came to Germany from Russia were sexual workers or those offering strategic information, but that was only for a couple of years before the leader changed sides. What do you specifically want to know though?"

"I need to find out why a woman of obviously Russian heritage might have a German accent during the war," Alric explained.

"Ah, well, it could be that she wasn't actually in Germany, but maybe from Poland, Hungary, or similar countries. A lot of them were 'resettled' post-war or invaded. If they were Jewish, the danger would have been extreme."

"So, while she may have a German accent that doesn't necessarily mean she's German?" he clarified.

"A person with that accent could be Austrian, even. Those countries had very changeable borders and it depended on which incarnation of ruling families too. It was a messy period of history." Sunny was heard rustling something. "There's lots of literature. I can send you some information if you want."

"No, that's fine." He nearly ended the call then stopped. "Wait, if someone was emigrating from those countries to say, Australia, what records would there be?"

"Oh, that I'm not able to tell you. But look, how soon do you need the information?"

His hand clutched the communicator. "As quickly as you can get it, Sunny."

She sighed. "Okay, give me a couple of hours to crash, I've pulled two all-nighters in a row in preparation for today's exam and I'm brain-fogged."

He wanted to scream at her to do it now. But he remembered the days of extreme exhaustion of being a student in the final year. Given it was late evening on the other side of the world, he felt a little guilty at annoying her. "Okay. Thanks, sunshine."

"Anything for you, brother mine. Now go away, I'm almost asleep here." And indeed her voice had taken on a soft and floaty quality.

He disconnected the call and turned to Nala. "Well?" he asked.

"Well, like Sunny said, she could be an immigrant. I remember we had to have paperwork, passports, and so on. Mum and Dad had problems when Edmund was almost born on the ship, and Mum was hospitalised when we landed. So according to the government, he was Australian, and that was that."

Alric grunted as he considered what she'd said. There had to be paperwork.

"Do we need to travel to Germany?" she asked, and he heard the trepidation in her voice.

"No, I don't think so. But there is a German section in town here. If she's looking for a bolt-hole, she might go there."

Nala nodded. "It may also be the place where we can lay a trap? That's what you're thinking, isn't it?"

His guts curdled at the thought. "One step at a time," he reminded her, hoping they may not yet need that option. "We need to check our video, see if that's a possibility. We'll need Eshant's people to do that, and quickly. If we can put together a good plan, one with a chance of success, we might be able to end this today."

She gazed at him, and he wondered if she understood his internal turmoil. "Whatever it takes then," she said.

He just hoped they could contain the woman before she struck again.

22

Nala followed Alric down the walkway from the mass transit system.

Eshant had come through, as the videos had indeed captured a person, dressed as Alric remembered, on the mass transit. Sarah had travelled to this area, and Nala and Alric discussed their plans.

"We aren't dealing with someone who's thinking logically, Nala."

Nala twisted a strand of hair around her finger and considered the video. "No. I think you're right, except in her mind, she's got a plan. She strikes me as someone who thinks she's got an iron-clad scheme."

"You're the one who knows her best, Nala. Is she likely to stay there for a few days?"

"I don't know. You must understand, for many of us, jaunting around the countryside wasn't something we were used to. You'd be born, grow, live, and die in a single region for most of the populace."

"So, there's a better than even chance that she's scouted out a location as her home base," he muttered to himself, and Nala watched the way his jaw tensed as he deconstructed what they knew. "We need Eshant now; we need people in place and a central location that will draw her out."

"How do we know…?"

"Her mentor mentioned that she'd taken to electronics, didn't he? Found her more than once watching the live cams, yes?"

Nala nodded.

"I'm willing to bet she found the cams for the German quarter and is keeping abreast of the comings and goings. Likely looking for any kind of increased attention from law enforcement."

The area they would investigate was known as the German quarter, and it reminded her of England, the buildings old and reminiscent of times gone by. "This area looks old," she said. "Most of the rest of the area is different. I guess, it's been rebuilt?"

Alric shook his head. "Kleindeutschland is a law unto itself, really. There were rallies and protests when it was suggested that it be part of the integrated rebuilding of New York about a century ago, if I remember correctly. It wasn't the first time either, there have been several attempts in the last couple of centuries, including after the 9/11 tragedy."

"9/11?"

He sighed, and it reinforced that it was another major historical fact that she'd not learned of. "It was a large terrorist action. Pilots crashing planes full of civilians into buildings. Shut air traffic down in the United States and created havoc."

She was shocked at the information, and her eyes rounded. "Oh!"

"Anyway, as I was saying, about three decades ago, the residents of Kleindeutschland protested and won. The government made this an area of historical significance and ensured a covenant was put in place to make sure it was never redeveloped."

"Wow. That amazes me. I mean, there are lots of places that have redeveloped and the hints of what was there before are gone. Though, a lot of that was because of the war, so…" She shrugged.

He pulled her along the sidewalk, toward a café. "Let's get a coffee, and we can watch people for a while."

"Sure," she agreed, though she wondered if this was his plan to draw Sarah out.

He dragged her to a table near the door. "This looks nice," he said as they settled under an umbrella.

"You want me on display?" She blinked while waiting for his response.

"Am I that transparent?"

"To me, yes. I don't think Sarah would necessarily get it. She's very self-involved, so me being here will be, as far as she's concerned, just an opportunity."

He moved inside, and she watched the crowd, looking for a hint that he may be right, that this is where she would have holed up.

Time passed as she fiddled with her communicator, but nothing caught her attention. Eventually, Alric returned. "The coffee will be out soon." He moved in closer, as if he were going to kiss her on the temple. "I'm going to head back inside, so I'll be close by. But I want you to be safe, my love. Take this." He pressed a small stunner into her hand. "Remain aware, she's obviously dangerous, and I have no intention of losing you now."

A tremor ran through her. "I promise I'll be careful." She shoved the stunner into the folds of her skirt, ensuring it was easily accessible.

"I have apprised Eshant, and he and his people are also milling around in the area," he whispered then disappeared back inside.

The concern inside her raged back into life. She knew this was the best option to try to get Sarah to show her hand. The coffee was delivered, and she sipped it, feeling the buzz of awareness, and wondering if that was her.

Her mouth dried as she waited in the sunshine, and just as she was sure there couldn't be any chance, a form separated itself from the crowd and headed toward her.

Looking up, Nala saw it was Sarah, and her stomach knotted. Alric had told her to toss her hair if she saw Sarah, so Nala complied, brushing it back, before sliding her hand down to her skirt so her fingers brushed against the stunner she held there.

Sarah settled into the chair opposite her. "Well, this is a surprise. I wouldn't have considered you would wander so far afield, Nala. You're too much of a mouse. But it seems I was wrong. You appear well, so I guess my earlier attempts weren't overly successful."

The woman opposite sprawled in the chair, with a nonchalant air.

"What is it you want, Sarah? Why are you hurting people?" Her voice wobbled, and while Nala wished she'd been able to sound normal, she knew Sarah picked up on the anomaly.

Sarah's smile was feral; cold and vicious.

The nerves in Nala's hand quivered and jumped, and she curled her hand around the handle of the stunner.

"I want what you have. A level of freedom that I wouldn't normally be able to achieve, Nala, and the only way to do that is to eliminate anyone who could get in my way."

"Is that why you killed Maxwell and Michaels?"

Sarah trilled with laughter. "Maxwell was an accident. It just happened."

"And Michaels?"

"He was an unnecessary distraction. An enjoyable one over the years, during my time as a hostess, but times change." She tittered. "It looks like you've found a distraction too. A good-looking one, but clearly, he is inattentive, to be leaving you alone." She smiled again. "Your loss and my gain."

Nala shivered at the frigid gaze. She'd only seen this kind of lack of empathy once, and that was in the institution during her nursing training. "So, what do you plan to do now, Sarah?"

"Do? That's simple, I need to neutralise you. I need what you have, and this is the only way to get it. It's not personal, Nala. I don't want to hurt you, but it's necessary, don't you see?"

Nala shook her head. "No, I honestly don't. You aren't me, so you can't have what I have, Sarah."

Sarah groaned dramatically. "No, you don't see, do you?" She ran her fingers through her hair. "Others never do."

Nala had the impression that Sarah was talking to herself, reinforcing what she thought.

"I know how to get what I want. I learned young how to plan and to put in place what needs to be done, and that is to remove you. That's what living in the war teaches you."

"No, Sarah. War teaches you to be resilient, but not how to kill others. There are other ways to cope with your impulses."

Those words galvanised Sarah, and Nala wanted to curse. "Don't! Don't talk to me about impulses." Sarah's nostrils quivered, and Nala hoped that the information she was gathering, the recording that both Eshant and Alric had, would be enough soon, because she was seriously unnerved by the discussion.

"What did I say wrong, Sarah?" Her hand shook.

"I know all about impulses. I know what happens to people with impulse issues. I've received treatment for that, and let me tell you," the other woman said, leaning forward, "I have no intention of facing that again." Sarah spoke harshly, spittle flying across the table.

"Anyway…" Sarah said calmly. In a flash, her attitude had changed, her face once more composed. She folded both her hands on the table before them, and for the first time, Nala saw the knife, long and serrated, that was in the woman's grip.

Nala gulped. "Don't do this, Sarah. Please." She knew she sounded terrified, but she needed to make the woman change her mind. She really didn't want to have to do what she'd be forced to do if Sarah continued. But entreaty was in vain.

Sarah smiled. "I don't usually like to have to act in such a public place, but needs must, and I doubt you'll go somewhere more private with me, would you?"

Then she moved like lightning, the knife flashing upwards, glinting in the sunlight.

Nala gasped, pointing the weapon and squeezing the trigger, just like Alric had showed her at the range.

Sarah cried out, the hand clutching the knife arched in the air. The woman shivered in shock as the stream of electricity caused chaos with her nerves.

Nala surged up, pushing away from the table as the chair dropped to the ground.

Bodies moved, like an intricately choreographed dance of synchronicity, toward the woman.

Hands grabbed Nala, ones she knew intimately. "Nala, are you okay? No injuries?" Alric's voice was panicked.

"I'm…" She clutched his hands. "I'm uninjured, but Alric, she needs help." Tears dribbled down her cheeks.

He pulled her against his body, his lips touching her temple. "Thank God," he whispered.

Alric had watched the woman talking, once he'd noted Nala's signal. He'd accessed the voice recorder, while Eshant sat beside him.

"You're sure she can handle this, Alric?"

He grunted. "She's capable and level-headed. Knows what we need."

Even so, his hands fisted as panic bubbled in his chest. He fought it back down, needing to concentrate, to be aware of when Nala needed him.

"What is it you want, Sarah? Why are you hurting people?" Nala's voice echoed, tinny, and sounded like she was a world away.

Sarah's voice was falsely high-pitched and grated on him as she answered with, "I want what you have. A level of freedom that I wouldn't normally be able to achieve, Nala, and the only way to do that is to eliminate anyone who could get in my way."

He almost rose when Nala began to explain why Sarah's demands were unworkable, but he waited, aware that the plans they'd made, and the extra precaution of the stunner, worked in Nala's favour.

Controlling his impulse to barge out there kept him in his spot until Sarah spat, "Don't! Don't talk to me about impulses."

"Don't interfere just yet," Eshant demanded as if he read what Alric needed to do.

"She's lost it though, Eshant. I'm not putting Nala in danger," he growled.

"You told me she could handle herself," the man reminded him, speaking mildly, fingers caressing the mug of coffee before him.

Alric wanted to hit the man, but contained the rage burning inside him, because he understood the necessity of waiting just a little longer.

Sarah's voice echoed, "I don't usually like to have to act in such a public place, but needs must, and I doubt you'll go somewhere more private with me, would you?"

Another voice came through the receiver, "Go! Go! Go!" And both he and Eshant were out of their chairs, across the room and through the door before his brain engaged that it was nearly done.

His brain demanded he move faster, while his heart was praying for Nala's safety. He grabbed her shoulder. "Nala, are you okay? No injuries?" Panic was a bubble in his chest, restricting his ability to breathe.

"I'm…" Her hands clutched at him, as if she were desperate for a lifeline. "I'm uninjured, but Alric, she needs help."

He pulled her against his body, his lips touching her temple, and he contained the instinctive shiver of reaction. "Thank God," he whispered and closed his eyes. Sent up a prayer of thanks to whoever was listening. "You should sit down," he muttered, because he needed to do the same. His legs felt like wet noodles, and suddenly the reality of the risk they'd taken swamped him.

They settled far enough away to watch safely as Sarah was apprehended.

"She'll be okay, won't she? I mean, I didn't kill her." Nala's whisper broke through the fugue surrounding him.

"She'll live," he muttered. Unlike those she's already murdered. He didn't say the words out loud, because it was clear Nala was suffering for the morning's work.

"What will happen to her now?" She turned toward him, her eyes pools of distress, tears obscuring her irises.

"Eshant," he called, aware that answering her questions was something he didn't have the specific knowledge of.

The man stalked toward them, settled on a chair. "What?"

"What will happen to her now?" Nala repeated her question, and the man frowned.

"It really depends on what we find as part of our ongoing investigation. She'll meet with a psychoanalyst. They will determine what medical or chemical intervention is necessary. She'll need to face charges for murder, that can't be forgotten."

Nala nodded. "I understand that, but what will be done for her? To her?"

"Likely incarceration, during which time she'll have opportunities for re-education. Her reintegration into society will be reliant on how well she takes that assistance and any medication, should that be part of a treatment plan. In the meantime, I'd bet that off-planet holding will be in her future." Eshant spoke without emotion, and Alric saw the pain on Nala's face at the description of Sarah's future.

Alric gripped her hand and noted that Eshant's gaze settled on that.

"Like that, I see. You do realise that mentors and designates are precluded—"

Narrowing his gaze, Alric met Eshant's stare. "And?"

He shrugged. "I'm not willing to say anything, just… Don't be too obvious, friend."

Alric growled. "I'd never call us friends."

Eshant's nod was slow. "I envied you, all those years ago, in the academy, you know. You were popular, and while your grades were good, you had that something extra that I knew I didn't."

Alric stilled. "What?"

Eshant turned to Nala. "I'm glad you're safe. Anyway, I must be away. Reports to write, as you know, Alric. Oh, and once you present your report and receipts, all costs will be reimbursed and you're free to continue your time. You've got, what? A week and a half?" He stood and walked away, calling to his men, who fell in behind him.

"I don't think he's half as officious as you said," Nala said quietly.

Alric watched as Eshant walked away. Maybe I've read the man wrong all those years. Maybe.

23

The chime of her communicator roused Nala from her doze. They'd arrived back at Alric's in the early afternoon, and she'd retired to what had become her room, to shower and rest, leaving Alric to get on with writing his report.

Pressing the button, she glanced at the message.

Application for specialist designate intake confirmed.

Nala sucked in a breath, scrolling through with shaking hands, reading the text, and her brain sluggishly accepted that she'd be undertaking specialist training in medicine. To be a doctor!

"I did it," she breathed, staring at the screen. A long-held dream was about to become a reality.

Bolting off the bed, uncaring whether her hair was in disarray, she hurried toward Alric's office, but stopped when she saw him. He looked wrung out. Exhausted.

Knocking, she waited for him to register her presence. "Nala! I came up to check on you earlier, but you were sleeping."

She smiled and entered the room. "You could have joined me," she said, but he shook his head.

"No. I had my report to complete, then an urgent communique

from the Captivar. My second-in-command… She left the ship yesterday and is now refusing to return." He pinched the bridge of his nose. "I knew when she was placed, this was a risk, but…" He shrugged. "The-powers-that-be made a mistake, and I have to go back and clean up the mess."

Shock punched into her. "Oh. Okay. So when do you leave, and where do you want me to go?"

He stood, rounded the table, and grabbed her shoulders. "I want you to come with me, Nala. I have to leave tomorrow morning, but I don't… Please, I don't want to lose what we have." There was a wealth of desperation in his voice.

"I…" How to answer that? "I want to go with you, but…" Her hand shook as she extended the communicator to him so he'd see the words.

He read them, then lifted his head. "This…" Alric cupped her cheek with a shaking hand. "I know you want this, but Nala, our training courses don't require you to be in any one location, you know that, right? You can study on the Captivar. Come with me, love."

Nala bit her lip, staring at him. Heaven knew she wanted to go with him, but she needed to be sure. She refused to use him as a crutch, something she'd seen far too much in her own time.

Clearing her throat, she shook her head, and his face paled, the brightness of his green eyes fading. "Not yet. I need time, Alric. I need to find out who I am in this time. What I can be." But the pain in her chest was crushing. "I'm not saying 'never,' just… not yet."

He nodded slowly and backed away.

"No, Alric." She reached out, grabbing his hand. "I want you and us. Don't confuse that with my wanting to stay here. Just I need time. I need to find how I belong, and I can't do that by clutching onto you like a limpet."

He didn't look at her, and she felt the hot sting of tears.

"Damn it, don't make this harder, Alric. I want to come with you. I do, but not yet. Give me six months. Time to establish myself, then if you still want me, I'll come, and gladly."

He turned back, eyes hooded. "I need to go pack."

"Don't lock me out, Alric." Panic was bubbling inside her. She was losing him, and she wasn't ready for that. "I... I think I..." She swallowed the words because she needed to be sure. There was no way she could give up the little bit of autonomy she'd clawed together on a wish or a hope or a maybe. He didn't deserve that, and neither did she. When she came to him, it would be as an equal in the relationship.

But he wasn't going to let her go so easily. "What, Nala? What were you going to say?"

"I'm not ready to put a name on what's between us. That's not fair to either of us, but I will tell you, I feel deeply for you. But I need this time, and if you care for me, you'll understand that."

He nodded though his mouth was tight and lined with white. "Alright then. Six months."

When he turned and ran an unsteady hand through his hair, she felt the chill of his withdrawal.

"Alric?" She stepped up to him. "I want to make love with you, if you would like." In her mind, it was like a last meal before she underwent a long period of starvation. Six months was a long time, but it was necessary, because she needed to be sure. Needed him to be sure.

He turned, taking her in his arms, the move lightning-quick, and his mouth descended to devour, to demand everything she had to give.

The embrace turned frenzied as he tore at her clothing. "I love every inch of you," he muttered as the last piece of clothing between them dropped to the floor.

Her body flamed, nerves desperate for the slide of skin against skin, and her brain urged her to give and take in equal measure. Lips roamed and fingers caressed as sighs and moans filled the air.

With a firm grip, he hoisted her to the edge of the desk, and once perched there, her legs encircled his waist. "Please," she muttered. "Love me, Alric."

"I already do," he crooned, then their bodies joined.

He moved, the rhythm carnally orchestrated to push them both to a climax that exploded.

Her eyes closed as he moved a last time, grunted, and stilled against her, his body pulsing with release.

"I love you, Nala," he muttered against her lips.

A single tear dribbled down her cheek. "I know," she answered.

EPILOGUE

Nala glanced at the notes before her.

Day one hundred and eighty-three.

Ninety-four calls.

Four hundred and twenty communications.

Six long months. Five months, three weeks, and six days too long, she thought, of waiting for the man she knew she loved to return to her. Because she'd demanded this time.

Swiping at the tears in her eyes, she waited, impatient for the hours to pass. He'd told her he'd arrive somewhere around lunch, and she'd dithered about, looking for the right clothes, preparing food.

What if he doesn't come? The panic kept raising its head, and she brushed it aside because he'd said he'd be there.

Her stomach wobbled as the sound of the door opening heralded Alric's return. It took every ounce of restraint to stay in the dining room as they'd agreed. The urge to rush to him, to grab him and...

He smiled at her as he entered the room, and now, she rushed, throwing herself into his embrace.

The kiss was sweet and all too brief. "I missed you," she breathed against his lips.

"God knows, I missed you too, Nala love. Six months is just too long."

"Good, because I've been thinking." She broke away from him, turned toward the hall and crooked her finger as she glanced over her shoulder. "But before that, I have something for you."

"Something for me? What?"

"Me!" she said and ran up the steps to his bedroom, the one he'd been insistent she should use in his absence.

He bounded up the steps, following her, capturing her waist, and swinging her into his arms before shoving open the bedroom door.

"Wait," she called, and he stopped, looking down at her, and she wiggled herself out of his grasp.

"What?" He appeared startled, and she grinned.

"Before we make love, I need to tell you a few things." She hurried to the wardrobe and pulled it open to show him an array of bright clothing. "The time apart? It let me find out who I can be, and I like who I've become." She whirled away, snatching up papers she'd purposely laid beside the bed. "Second, I've done so well in my training that I'm being allowed to specialise early and will be placed on the Captivar as part of my advanced interstellar and space-related trauma studies. Where you go, I can go. And it allows me to work in an area of need."

With a final smile, she stepped up to him, launching herself into his embrace.

"Lastly? I know the truth. I love you." As she waited for his reaction, it felt as if a boulder had stopped her breathing, but that feeling melted away as the smile on his face expanded to a delighted grin.

"Love me, huh? That's good, because I've missed you so much, Nala. And I love you too."

This time the kiss ignited the flame she'd kept banked inside herself for six months.

For five months, three weeks, six days, and twenty-three hours she'd missed him, and finally the wait was over.

The End
For Now

THE BLOOD BRIDE BY IMOGENE NIX

Hope just wants to be an ordinary nestling. She went to college and escaped, but now she's back and there's a secret everyone is keeping from her.

Xavier is the new master of the nest, ready to welcome home the daughter of the house who he has never met. He's unprepared for the woman who steals his breath and enchants him.

Now Hope and Xavier must fight for lives and those of the innocents. After all, it is only by overcoming the rogues that they will have a chance of a timeless future together. But will it be in time?

PROLOGUE

As silence descended on the house, the shadows grew—dark grays and blacks that bled into each other. First one figure then another broke away, making a run toward the house. Silent as the grave, they moved swiftly over dew-slicked grass. Then they stopped still. Waiting. Not a movement betrayed them until a signal propelled them back into action and they started crawling upwards. The walls damp coating no barrier to the intruders that ascended in the darkness.

The sound of each window breaking shattered the quiet—the figures were inside. Screams echoed through the night. Yet, in this area of large estates, heavy with noise-absorbing shrubbery, no one could hear those within. The blood-curdling screams went on and on before finally dying away.

Just one sound echoed through the night: The sobbing of a child.

The front door opened and figures trooped out—ghostly specters against an inky night sky, broken by a single outline. A child in white, carried at the center of the pack.

No sound broke the silence as they moved toward the trees surrounded the house.

Flames now licked at the manor: A deathly glow of oily smoke rising.

All that remained was a single person—wrapped in a cape of midnight blue beyond the house—watching them melt away.

Jemima moved toward the burning structure, breaking into a run as she breached the threshold. Vainly she attempted to enter, but the heat drove her back.

Now dashing tears from her face, she raced across the graveled driveway toward the gates, where the guardhouse was located. No sign of life existed within the building and some instinct of survival slowed her pace to a careful creep. Out of breath and heaving from exertion, she nervously checked within.

Small puffs of white vapor colored the glass. She darted from one window to another. Her cloak drawn tightly around her body, hoping it would camouflage her from sight.

Satisfied, Jemima entered through the heavy, wooden front door and moved toward the phone she spied on the floor. Her eyes darting here and there she dialed, listening to the rotary motor as it returned to the proper position. Time was short and if *they* came back, she needed to have shared the message.

The phone rang once. Twice. With a brrping sound it connected.

"Hello?" A male answered and she felt a warm flush of relief at the voice. A voice she knew well.

"The manor has been breached. The girl child taken." The words erupted and her hand trembled.

"On our way." The click of the receiver being replaced echoed loudly in the stillness of the room.

Copper. She smelled copper.

Her stomach soured, knowing it meant more deaths. Jemima looked around for the gun—a gun with deadly, holy water-infused copper bullets—she knew was hidden somewhere in the room. A gun she couldn't find. *No divine intervention exists here,* she thought.

Hopefully *they* didn't remain. Feeding. If they were still here, that's what they would be doing. She found a corner and scrunched down, hiding from sight.

Crouched low, she tried to stay as still as possible, listening for sounds of the vehicles she knew would be coming. She dug her fingers into the flesh of her arms; remaining aware enough to stop before drawing blood. That would surely bring them out. Jemima dragged the cloak around her to capture the warmth, yet there was little to be found.

The sounds of engines roused her from the corner of the room. Jemima inched toward the window, the lead of the old glass distorting her view, hearing raised voices she knew Mistress Cressida had arrived.

Jemima retreated. Remained hidden from the woman because if she knew, all may well be lost. From the shadowed room she listened to the conversation...

"It smells like Estersham." The Mistress' eyes closed. "If it is, we have a problem." She turned once more, her face set and eyes now glacial in intensity. "James?"

The man nodded as if he knew what was to come.

"If I take those steps, I cannot return. Another must stand in my place." Her voice hardened while her eyes glittered in the dim light, piercing in their intensity.

Then the Mistress' voice called out in the near silence. "You and yours have been my loyal servants for so many years. I took an oath to protect you long ago. I renewed it with marriage and births, over and over. Now, my home and yours have been breached and this child taken from us. The girl child, who will be the hope and salvation of our kind, was ripped from the bosom of our nest. I will repay your loyalty and I will get her back." The words of power rippled in the night and licked at Jemima's skin.

Available in Ebook
books2read.com/BloodBride-Nix

Direct Autographed Copy
https://www.imogenenix.net/BloodBride

THE RESET

A zombie apocalypse is here, but figuring out how to survive in the immediate aftermath is only the first step.

Elaine is just an ordinary woman, but when the apocalypse occurs, she must find a way to survive in an increasingly hostile world. Enter Liam, the policeman who saves her at their first meeting and provides assistance as they try to cope with the zombie outbreak brought about by an unknown infection that's spreading out of control.

Together they form a community, trying to save as many lives as they can, a place where people can be safe. Even in the throes of disaster though, emotions creep up, taking both of them by surprise. Who knows? They might just get their happy ever after…if they can survive.

Elaine's fingers curled over the radio, her heart stuttering with fright.

"Officials are unable to determine the cause of the illness breaking out all over the city, but urge calm. If you are cornered by the infected, seek safety. Should you be bitten, seek medical attention immediately."

Her fingers fluttered against her lips. The dirge rose, long moans as those infected, their skin turning a deep grayish green and their eyes milky white, howled outside the office. Elaine pushed the curtain aside once more and glanced through the glass. The collection had grown, their faces slack yet eerily aware that she remained inside.

"I don't know what to do." She turned back to watch as her boss, William Eckerman, rocked in his seat. "I mean, we've been holed up here for over two days. There's no food in the kitchenette, the toilet is overflowing, and we can't stay here, otherwise we'll die." The jitter of her stomach warned her that panic was rising up, about to overwhelm her.

"Elaine, relax. It's just a precautionary measure. The police will come and…"

"The police have indicated that they are overwhelmed. Military forces are on the way, but communications are hampered by the…by the walking dead converging on sites with power. In the latest update, the government is ceasing all non-urgent tasks. They're recommending that you hunker down and hope you can ride it out. Resources are limited, and it's suggested that, if possible, you should stock up and find a safe location in which to secure yourself." The announcer's voice shook.

"See? They're saying we need to find a secure location, stock up, and hide. Mr. Eckerman, we can't stay here." The urge to flee coursed through her veins like an exploding freight train. "We have to go to our homes. Be with our families."

He flicked invisible specks of lint from his immaculate sleeves and rocked again in the seat. "Well, Elaine, I think, given your current level of excitation, you should certainly go home."

She frowned at the cool tone. "Uhhh, Mr. Eckerman?" "Yes?"

"Mr. Eckerman—"

"When this is over, I'll give you an excellent reference for the four years of service. It's sad that something has overset you to the point where completing your work is no longer your priority. I understand it is probably time to expand your employment horizon."

As she stood there listening to the drivel he was spouting, growing anger warred with her terror. "Mr. Eckerman..."

"Go on and get your things together. It's best you go directly home."

She shuffled to her desk, shock assaulting her as she gathered the few personal items she'd stashed. The photo of her parents, the Mickey Mouse cup she'd bought at a major attraction. The hairbrush and small clutch of cosmetics joined the rest of her belongings, then Elaine straightened, turned, and headed for the door.

"Aren't you forgetting something?" Mr. Eckerman held out his hand, and she blinked. "Umm, what?"

"Keys."

She blinked again then made an 'O' with her mouth. "I forgot them when I came in. I'll have to drop them off once everything is done."

He snarled and opened the door. "Go on then. I want them back here as soon as the situation is cleared."

She looked outside, glad he'd insisted on staff using the back door, which was protected by the security fencing and remote-controlled roller door. She hurried to her vehicle, pleased it was older and heavier, sure it would protect her until she reached home.

Leaving the building was scarier than she expected. As she drove the short distance she constantly glanced around, seeing small huddles here and there of those who were infected. Each time they lurched in her direction she panted, heartrate increasing, adrenaline spiking until she was past them.

Turning onto her street left her amazed. Smoking wrecks of cars littered the street, and several gray-skinned individuals loitered. She drove carefully, hoping she could make it home without being waylaid.

When she reached her house she swung in to park on the road, thinking she'd have plenty of time to get in the house without any of the walkers in the way. She found the key for the front door, checked the rearview mirror to make sure none of the infected were close by, then got out of the car. Slamming the car door shut, she engaged the locks and sprinted to her front door.

Fighting the jamb until the door eased open, Elaine slid within and pushed the door shut. The tiny house on the outskirts of town she shared with her best friend had a deserted feel to it.

"Emily?" Once sure the door was securely latched she hurried up the hall, calling her friend's name. Every door she opened and peered inside was empty, and at the end of ten fruitless minutes she slumped down in a kitchen chair.

Liam wasn't sure what to do. The supermarket was empty, and shelves of food were scattered on the floor as he picked his way along the aisles.

"They said to lay in supplies then hunker down." He glanced at the phone in his hand. "They didn't say to break into the supermarket though." Ramon, his half-brother, snickered into the camera of the phone, and Liam shrugged.

They'd flown into Canberra three days ago and settled into the tiny B-and-B on the edge of this township. The location seemed great, only a few miles from Parliament House. It was close to the venue of the three-day conference he was attending on policing in emergency situations. Ramon had come because he'd concluded his last contract in an African country with a bubonic plague epidemic and was at a loose end.

No one could have expected something like this outbreak to occur though, and food was a priority. Liam had insisted Ramon stay at the B-and-B. Having a brother who was an epidemiologist and infection prevention specialist meant he might be called upon by the authorities for assistance, and they couldn't afford for him to be infected by the virus.

"Okay, I'll see what I can find and get back there as quickly as I can." Liam disconnected the call and turned to scan the shelves. "Long-life milk, because it will be good for at least a year on the shelf, sugar, coffee. Bottled water. Some powdered milk as well." He thrust them into the trolley and moved as quickly as he could toward the end of the aisle.

A groan stilled him. He'd already seen the results of those infected, the way they set upon victims, the dripping, bloody teeth. If that moan was anything to go by, he was no longer alone in the shop.

"Get back!" The startled words of a woman almost had him jumping.

"Hello?" He cursed inwardly for now making himself a target as the sound of shambling footsteps echoed, moving in his direction.

"He's heading your way!" the woman yelled as the gray man turned the corner, eyes blank, mouth slack through dripping trails of scarlet. The outstretched hands moved toward him. He didn't have anything on him that would be considered a weapon and cursed that decision. The paperwork for going armed in public—something the department had been cracking down on lately—would have been worth it after all.

The creature extended its arms and gave an "uhhh" sound, and he pondered for a moment whether there was some way to disable it. The thought came and went when the woman screamed and a second and third shuffler made its way in his direction.

The handle of the trolley was just in reach and he tugged it backward, braced his legs, then ran in the direction of the shuffler. The trolley hit the creature in the chest, and it went down, legs and arms waving frantically until it rolled. Now the sound that emanated from its mouth became more of a growl of fury.

He reached out, his hand curling around the nearest can. Saying a silent prayer, he aimed and threw. The crack of heavy metal on bone and the spray of blood as the man went down without a whimper gave him momentary pleasure, but not before the woman from the next aisle scurried around to him.

"There's two more," she screamed.

He didn't glance at her, merely reached up, grabbed another tomato soup can, and lobbed. It hit without the power to cease the onward march.

"Dammit!"

"I've... There's some kitchen string here. Would that help?"

He turned briefly and acknowledged the beautiful, curvy, red-haired woman thrusting the plastic-wrapped item at him, but he shook his head as they stumbled backward.

"We're going to need something a little more useful." He considered what might be here in this tiny store as the woman disappeared before returning with two long, metal-headed rakes. "What about these?" she asked.

He laughed, grabbed one out of her hands as the walkers came within reach, and thwacked it down hard on the head of the nearest one. The rake dropped with a thud and rolled under the shelving unit.

She made a sound, rather like a moan, and turned away as he snatched the other implement and used it to push the other shuffler back.

This time he lined up the male, sidestepped its attempt at grabbing him, then swung this new rake like a bat. The infected individual fell to the floor, and he brought the rake down on its head. She turned and retched while he waited.

"They're... Those were humans! Why did you—"

"No, they aren't humans anymore. They were zombies, and they'll kill you as soon as look at you. Now grab what you need so we can get out of here."

He glanced down one last time at the remains he'd left on the floor. He felt bad about what he'd had to do, but sugarcoating the truth wouldn't make it any better. The only thing they could do was stock up and get back to safety.

He threw tins and jugs into the trolley, along with frozen items, which he was sure would only be available for a little while longer. He also tossed in other essentials such as toilet rolls. He noted that the woman, tears flowing down her cheeks, followed his lead.

Then, with both trolleys full, they left the store and headed to the carpark. This was the danger time. He pulled out his cellphone and dialed Ramon. "Hey, I've got a full load and I'm heading in."

"Good, 'cause I'm hungry and the radio is just repeating what we already know."

He turned to the woman. "Will you be all right to get home?"

She sniffled inelegantly and nodded. "I'm just over the road there." She pointed to the

tiny cottage beside the B-and-B residence where he was staying, and he laughed. When she glanced at him, he sobered. "I'm right next door."

"Oh."

Available from Love Books Publishing
https://books2read.com/Reset

Direct Autographed Copy
https://imogenenix.net/product/the-reset/

A VERY MERRY WIDOW

A Very Merry Widow

Louisa thought she'd made the right choice. Jeremy had been the man she'd loved, but he wasn't who she thought he was. After he dies in a horse riding accident, she wants more. Not another husband, but perhaps a lover who'd fulfilled her needs while she raised her daughters.

Albert never expected to return to England, let alone to take up the family seat or the title of Earl of Conney. Yet here he was, returning from the wilds of Australia, with his friend, Frederick. A convicted felon. He'd sworn to himself if he was going to assume the title, he'd use the influence that went with it to clear his friends name. Brothers-in-law, Langdon Devereaux and Aeddan Fitzsimmons are the connections he needs, and they bring him into the contact with Louisa Lavenwood, a beautiful and aloof widow with two gorgeous but young daughters.

But she has a dark secret, and this unwilling hero feels the need to save her. Along the way passion explodes and they're helplessly lost in its thrall; if only they can overcome the danger, then perhaps more than passion lies in their future.

———————————

Louisa watched as the casket containing the body of her husband, Jeremy, was lowered into the ground. His coffin of dark oak and silver fittings shone in the weak daylight, and emotional numbness filled her senses. The fog of the morning had lifted a little, but the cold seeped into her bones as she dragged the heavy, black shawl close around her shaking body. The sounds of weeping from her mother-in-law beside her had been her companion since the accident. Now with the funeral passed, there was only the wake left to survive, then she could consider what came next. Where her future lay.

Her hand, clenched in a black kid glove, was slightly obscured by the black mourning veil she wore as she wiped at her cheek, hoping they'd not look too closely and know. Black would be the only colour she'd wear for a year because convention dictated it, followed by another year of grey, half-mourning. She hated knowing that she would be restricted again.

The bombazine of her gown, heavy and stiff, dragged at her body as her mind whirled with everything and nothing.

Since Jeremy's death, so many emotions had enveloped Louisa, but she'd held them tight within her breast.

Fury that he'd been so stupid as to be riding in a storm.

Grief that the man she'd loved had been taken from her.

But most of all, *betrayal*, because she knew who he'd been with.

There was more, she just knew it, but hadn't yet had time to enquire of her family's man of business. A man like Jeremy, one who'd lied to her face, who'd strayed just days before she gave birth... The truth was coming out, and she welcomed it with a vicious stab of honesty.

A storm was brewing—rage growing—and if *her ladyship* thought she'd simply keep quiet and sweet, she was in for a startling awakening. The roiling fury had grown in the last three days, and she promised herself that soon, she'd release the poison and begin to heal.

As soon as the requirements of widowhood were done, Louisa told herself as her eyes stung.

Exhaustion dragged at her weary mind.

She barely heard the words of the minister, committing her husband's remains to the ground.

All she knew was, with a child and a newborn babe, she was a widow. Alone in a man's world.

A hand reached out, took hers. *Elspeth*. Both her sisters, Isabelle and Elspeth and their husbands had made the trek back to the family home to support her when she needed them most. Men who were well-born. Men who she hoped would protect her from her mother-in-law's vicious tongue. Men who would protect her while she learned what she needed to know and while she decided what her future would look like.

Now wasn't the time to explain. There hadn't been time to do so before the funeral, but once Jeremy's family left, her sisters and brothers-in-law would hear all. It wouldn't be pretty, but she'd need their support. To make plans. Not just for herself but also her daughters.

Dirt was pressed into her hands, and she glanced down at it. "You need to throw it," Elspeth muttered.

She followed the instruction without a word, crouching down to ensure it thudded on the lid of the casket. Then she stayed there for a moment, silently considering. Finally, she rose.

The minister extended his hands. "I'm so very sorry for your loss."

She whispered something. It was probably the right words, but right now, she held tight to her control, the only thing that had bolstered her for the last few days. Ever since learning of Jeremy's betrayal and death.

At the gate, the carriages waited, one for her and her sisters. Their husbands would ride beside the jet-black conveyance. Another waited for Jeremy's grieving parents, and the rest of the family who'd attended had arranged their own transport.

Walking to the vehicle, silence echoed, apart from the cry of a crow. The sound crass and discordant.

Awareness that his family followed was cloying. Freedom was what Louisa craved most right now. Her sisters would surely see that and understand.

It was only once they were settled inside the carriage and it was moving that she took their hands. "Thank you for coming, sisters. We must talk. But after his family leaves." Her voice sounded scratchy from the night before, sobbing into the pillow that still faintly echoed the scent of Jeremy.

"Of course we would come." Isabelle patted her hands.

"You needed us, so we're here," Elspeth offered.

Looking at her sisters, both married with their own children, and returned to England, she wondered if she'd been too young. Too innocent. Too unaware when she'd accepted Jeremy. Thoughts of that day, the gown she'd worn, and the flush of success had gulled her into accepting a flawed man.

Her sisters had been initially concerned but had relented after she'd told them she wanted no one else. They acquiesced and as a young girl of seventeen she'd married Jeremy.

Now at twenty-three, she was a widow in black.

Jeremy's family had finally left as the night drew in. Dinner was quiet in the formal dining room; the staff brought her favourite—a solid and warming meal. The staff, even now, stood with her, protecting her as did her own family. Now, settled around the large fire in the parlour, she would tell them everything.

Isabelle and Elspeth crowded in beside her. Warming her more effectively than the fire could, while their husbands, Aeddan and Langdon, filled the wing chairs. They were strong, reliable men, and the right partners for her sisters, Louisa knew.

"What do you wish to tell us, dearest?" Elspeth gripped her hands.

"He… Jeremy. The night of the accident? He'd been out. There was a tremendous storm which blew in and he ventured home in it. But he'd… He had a mistress, Elspeth. A woman in the neighbouring township. He'd been with her."

Silence descended on the room. "You're sure?" Aeddan leaned forward, imbuing the question with power.

"Yes. I received a note yesterday. Before your arrival." She fished about in the pocket of her gown and drew it out with shaking hands. "Here, read it for yourself."

She didn't wish to ever see it again. The memory imprinted on her mind.

Dear Mrs Lavenwood,

Allow me to offer my condolences. Dearest Jeremy and I were as close as any man and woman could be. He confided in me, prior to the accident, that your recent interesting state and the doting on your daughter were difficult for him. He was a man who needed to be first in everything, including your affections, especially given his unfortunate position at birth.

However, it is my expectation that a token of his regard will be forthcoming to me. My expenses do not end with Jeremy's death as there is a child. As such, I feel it is only right, in light of the closeness we shared, that I should be granted a portion of his fortune, which I understand he personally used to purchase your family home.

I will, of course, be more than willing to engage with your solicitor at a time that is convenient to him.

Lady Pamela Jezerey

Aeddan swore and thrust the paper to Langdon, whose eyes glittered with fury as he read the missive. The paper then was read by both Elspeth and Isabelle.

"He had no claim on the house?" Aeddan queried. "So, he cannot gain any control of the Forster Shipping money or property?"

Elspeth shook her head. "When we drew up the marriage settlement, both Isabelle and I ensured the house did not pass from the family's control, nor any of the business. Louisa was young, and it was the best way we could protect her. The portion that went to Louisa was significant, but was not used in any way for the upkeep of the house or to pay the staff. They were all in the employ of Forster Shipping."

Langdon smiled. "And of course, he duly signed that?"

"Oh yes," Isabelle said with a smile. "We had our man of business bring in a senior solicitor from London to ensure everything was watertight. We love our sister." She shrugged then turned to Louisa. "We wanted to ensure her needs and those of any children were protected."

Aeddan stood and stalked to the fireplace, looked at it for a long moment. "With regards to this child this woman is claiming is your husband's. Has anyone questioned the veracity of her claim? That the child..."

Langdon nodded. "Yes, I agree. We need to establish if indeed the child was Jeremy's."

"No. I don't wish you to do that. Not openly or behind my back." Too many things had occurred, things Louisa knew nothing about until now, and she'd not allow anyone to hide this kind of information from her. Never again.

"But dearest," Elspeth stated, but stilled as Louisa shook her head.

"But you should know, Louisa. If the child *is* his... His parents should take some kind of steps."

Her laugh was discordant. "No, they won't. If this child is his, it's a bastard..." She huffed, because she knew that sounded callous. "I don't know the right answer, but if I've learned anything during this time, it's that his family shies away from truths that do not conform with their norm. Now then, I need to make decisions. Good decisions."

"But the child..." Isabelle leaned in. "It's innocent. It should be protected."

Louisa shook her head. "If there's a child, and I don't know the answer, what if it's not his?"

"Then we find out," answered Langdon. "Once the truth is known, then you can make a decision."

Louisa bit her lip, hearing for the first time the truth in his words. "Find out then," she whispered. "If it's not..."

"You have no responsibility," answered Isabelle.

"Perhaps now is the time to travel up to our properties," Elspeth added. "Take some time away while this is—"

Louisa inhaled deeply, felt the air in her chest, and prepared herself mentally. "Elspeth, much as I would love to run away from all this, you've both sheltered me for far too long. It's time I stood on my own. Took control of my life. I intend to see this through and to become an equal shareholder in Forster Shipping. I have two daughters who need to see their mama as an independent woman, and for too long, I allowed others to direct my life and felt secure in the lack of knowledge. If I've learned nothing else, it's that I'm strong and capable."

Louisa sat upright in the chair and stared forward at first one then the other sister.

When they both opened their mouths to remonstrate, Louisa held up a hand. "No. It's true. I will no longer be passive, sisters. I will see this mess of Jeremy's through, and as for Jezerey, well, whatever you learn will be dealt with by the solicitors. There is a full year of black, then when I can wear other colours. This is the time when I will consider my options."

This new Louisa was merely the tip as plans and ideas were unveiling in her mind. Not yet fully formed, but beginning to cascade. *I need time.* Time to let go of the dream, time to formulate her plan, and time to unravel the threads of a life barely lived before she could decide what and who the new Louisa would be.

"Living here? It's no longer enough, and I will need your support soon. Lady Constance is most insistent I should move to the Hall…" Before her sisters could speak, Louisa held up a hand. "…which I have no intentions of doing. She plans to take control of me and my life and my daughters' lives too. That I will not tolerate. Just as I will not tolerate her waspish friends and their whispers."

"We'll put paid to the biddies, my love," Elspeth answered. "You'll have our unwavering support and those of our circle. All you need to do is ask."

"Good," she said. "Because I've already sent for our man of business and the solicitor from London. I will stand on my own two feet, and I will protect what is mine and ours."

Available from Love Books Publishing
https://books2read.com/MerryWidow

Direct Autographed Copy
https://imogenenix.net/product/a-very-merry-widow/

ALSO BY IMOGENE NIX

<u>Warriors of the Elector</u>

- Star of Ishtar
- Starline
- Starfire
- Star of the Fleet
- Starburst
- The Star of Eternity

The Star of Ishtar & Starline - Print

Starfire & Star of the Fleet - Print

Starburst & The Star of Eternity - Print

<u>Blood Secrets</u>

- The Blood Bride
- The Illuminated Witch
- The Sorcerer's Touch

<u>The Secrets World:</u>

<u>Blood Secrets</u>

- The Blood Bride
- The Illuminated Witch
- The Sorcerer's Touch

<u>House Secrets</u>

- As Dawn Breaks
- Immortal Consequences
- Edge of Night

All That Glitters - a House Secrets Novella

<u>Danu's Secrets</u>

- The Downfall of Padraic O'Shaunessy
- A Demon Called Grace
- The Secrets of Danu

<u>The Automaton Series</u>

- Haven House
- Nobel Crest

<u>The Search Duology</u>

- Miss Elspeth's Desire
- Miss Isabelle's Craving

<u>Duology World Novels</u>

- A Very Merry Widow

<u>Reunion Trilogy</u>

- War's End
- The Assassin
- Executing Justice

The Reunion Trilogy in Paperback

<u>Sex Love & Aliens</u>

- Tangled Webs
- False Webs
- Covert Webs

<u>21st Testing Protocol</u>

- Cyborg: Redux
- Children Of A Greater Evil
- When Evil Came To Stay
- Finis: The War To End All Wars

<u>Celtic Cupid Trilogy</u>

- Blame The Wine
- A Stranger's Embrace
- Revenge On Cupid

The Celtic Cupid Trilogy in Paperback

<u>Zombieology</u>

- The Reset
- I Dream of Zombies
- The Six Million Dollar Zombie
- Make Room For Zombies
- Days of Our Zombies
- Unnamed Zobiology title

<u>Out Of Time Series</u>

- Flight In time (coming in 2025)
- Bound In Time (coming in 2026)
- Running Out of Time (coming in 2026)

<u>Knights of Pleasure</u>

- Silken Knights

<u>Single Titles</u>

The Chocolate Affair (also in Print)

Falling In Love Again (Previously A Sapphire For Karina)

BioCybe (also in Print)

Hesparia's Tears (also in Print)

Tomorrow's Promise (also in Print)

A Bar In Paris (also in Print)

Inheritance Of The Blood (also in Print)

The Plan (also in Print)

Loving Memories (also in Print)

Hero of Heartbreak Hill (also in Print)

My One & Only (also in Print)

Curse Bound (also in Print)

<u>Non Fiction</u>

Self Publishing: Absolute Beginners Guide (With Suzi Love)

<u>Written as Ciara Cave</u>

25 Curated Ways To Get Rid Of Telemarketers

Book Signings for Absolute Beginners

ABOUT THE AUTHOR

Imogene is published in a range of romance genres including Paranormal, Science Fiction and Contemporary. She is mainly published in the UK and USA.

In 2010, Imogene Nix (the pen name not Imogene herself) was born. Imogene sat down and worked tirelessly for 3 months culminating in the book Starline, which became the first in a trilogy titled, "Warriors of the Elector." Since then she's had over 30 titles published and is now focusing on hybridising herself - with a mixture of traditionally published and self-published works.

In fact, she's taking control of many of her back catalogue books, which are slowly re-releasing as self-published titles.

Imogene is a member of a range of professional organisations world wide, and believes in the mantra of mentoring and paying it forward and is actively involved in mentorship (through NaNoWrimo and her vlog: In The Chair With Imogene Nix) and tutoring of new and upcoming authors.

In her spare time she loves to drink coffee, wine & eat chocolate and is parenting her spoiled dog and a ferocious cat along with her husband and daughter and looks forward to weekends away with her husband in their caravan "The Seven Year Hitch!" Do look forward to her caravan romance at some point!

Lastly, Imogene returned to University during the pandemic and in 2023 completed her Master of Communication and now is enrolled in her PhD... She's a glutton for punishment, but never fear, imogene continues to write and publish books for readers to enjoy!

To Contact Imogene
www.imogenenix.net
imogene@imogenenix.net

Sign up for her newsletter at
https://www.imogenenix.net/Signup

facebook.com/ImogeneNix
x.com/ImogeneNix
instagram.com/ImogeneNix
bookbub.com/authors/imogenenix